To Wayne,
Thank you for the supp[ort]
it means so much for [someone]
like me just starting ou[t]

Emily Sutcliffe

The Elephant
in the Room

Emily Sutcliffe

Eloquent Books
New York, New York

Eloquent Books
An imprint of Writers Literary & Publishing Services, Inc.
845 Third Avenue, 6th Floor – 6016
New York, NY 10022

http://www.strategicbookpublishing.com

ISBN: 978-1-60860-557-6

Printed in the United States of America

Contents

In memory of my Dad
John Patrick Sutcliffe

Chapter One

He could hear her when she walked about above him, uninhibitedly unaware that he listened for her footsteps across his ceiling. He had to become very still, like stone. She was such a lithe shadow, a ghost, haunting his awareness. When he slept, he dreamt nightmares; a past he couldn't leave behind though he would try so desperately to. He slept rarely, afraid for what he wanted to forget to halt his progress now, such that it was. It was when he first heard her above him as he stared at his ceiling, willing the night to wane. Her patter came like whispers and lulled his quiet persecution, gifting him a tiny measure of peace from his demons, as redeeming as they were relentless.

So he came to listen for her and came to know the routine of her hours like his own. When he did sleep, he would wake when she woke and follow the echo of her stirring on his ceiling as though the tiles were made of glass. Then she would leave, as she did every morning, and he would press his face up to the peephole in his door and watch her descend down the stairs and pass the distorted blear of his view. As though she was caught in some moment of time, every day she would pull a scarlet coat about her shoulders and every day she left and returned with a paper satchel with a lone baguette sticking out the top. Her hair was always the same, thick russet waves cut just above her shoulders; her skin was white as milk and splashed with freckles; and her eyes were always on the floor at her feet, so even now he didn't know their color. But he knew every curve of her slight frame, the shape of the features of her soft, sallow face, and the elegant curl of her fingers wreathed about the bushels she cradled as lovingly as an infant.

But most of all he knew her sadness, the quiet desperation of her footsteps, as though even while above him in the refuge of her own home, she was trying not to make a sound, trying to fool the world into forgetting she existed.

He knew her name only by what was listed beside the buzzer to her flat: R. LaMotte. He dared not imagine what the R could stand for.

When she would glide as she did, so graceful like she floated, and shadow the stoop of his door, he would cross to the window and wait until she appeared on the street below. Every day, like an explorer, she would walk in a different direction, her head turned down to the cobble-patched sidewalk, the sun, if it were shining, catching her hair like ravels of milky copper. He would watch her until she disappeared and only then would his day begin, only then would errands be tended and words written and his life, such as it was and what little he knew of it, unfold.

Chapter Two

The day had begun just like the last. Finn watched a weak sun clawing through the fog that had settled over the city like a blanket. If he stood on the tips of his toes, he could see a sliver of the river, sparkling like blue diamonds in the chill of the morning. The city had yet to wake and Finn savored these sparse moments when the street below was empty and the windows in the buildings he faced were still dark. At moments like this one he could pretend they were the only two people awake while all the world was sleeping.

His night had been restless, spent staring into the lifeless face of his computer monitor, pleading for the words to spark off his tongue and onto his fingertips, pleading for the words of a story that had no end, a story that he wasn't even sure had a middle act. But it did have a beginning. He knew it well and it cursed his prayers for peace and kept his closet sealed with the skeletons he could not rid himself.

Finn yawned long and hard and stretched his lanky, sinewy limbs. He tousled his stiff mop of black hair and it stuck up on end. His dark eyes were fogged over with sleep, like hot breath on a cold window pane, and when he tried to rub the weariness out on his fingertips, it only served to smear the blear over his cinnamon-colored irises.

He had been trapped at the same place in the chronicle for months. 'November in Berlin' was what it read, was the threshold he couldn't cross, afraid as he was spiteful to face again the demons he had left there. They waited for him and stalked his weaknesses like scavengers apt to pounce the moment his failing reared its ugly head again. They thought it inevitable and Finn, for all the fight he still possessed, was beginning to believe them. Perhaps he had outstayed his welcome here. Perhaps it was time again to move on, before the brute of his memories caught up to him. He tried to think up a reason, a reason other than her, for why he had remained so long here in the first place. He knew no one. But then neither, it appeared, did she. She left alone, returned the same, and never had he heard another pace of footsteps shadowing the frail specter of her own.

They were two lost souls and, for a reason unbeknownst to Finn, he was obligated to look out for her as only one misplaced being can for another. There were times he thought she knew that too, times, more often of late, that she would seem to look from the sidewalk at her feet and up into the glossy vast of his window, like she knew he was there, shadowing the haunt of her silent wander, and was appeased by the company.

It was such exquisite agony. It kept the peril of his listing existence alive and the pain of his imprisoned sorrow just numb enough for him to stay the insurgence of his lurking psychosis.

Capsized in his own mind, the suddenness with which Finn realized her footsteps had ceased startled him, and he took giant strides to reach the door just in time to see her fleet shadow drift passed. In the hook of her arm she cradled a stack of inky newspapers. Every day when she left, she left with another cluster, the leavings of a neighbor who went round the city collecting all the papers he came across in every language and the next day discarded them on the stoop of his door. Finn wondered if *he* ever wondered how the bushels seemed to disappear. With such care she carried them, like they were a baby, bundled within folds of shuffled parchment.

The ruby dye of her coat always snagged his eye like silk on a thorn, like a flashlight in the dark. Reason made him think she would have to compensate somehow for the dourness of every day. He saw her aglow with a vividness that must rage just beneath her freckle-speckled skin. He wished she would stand still long enough so he could trace the spatters of blush red like the veins of a puzzle.

Finn stepped back from the threshold, lingered a moment in weary limbo, then fetched his jacket off its hook and opened the door. He shut it softly at his back and jumped with a start when he looked up and the door across the hallway from his swung open. A short, willowy woman with strawberry blond hair and round, cerulean blue eyes emerged and a smile as brilliant as a mouthful of diamonds lit up her face.

"Hello, Finn," she said. She had a voice that was sugary and lamb's wool soft, like a tonic of liquid silk.

Finn smiled uneasily back at her.

"Hey, Dovey," he said. His manner had abruptly turned very anxious. Dovey gazed warmly at him but he stared instead at the multicolored gem broach pinned to the lapel of her tan-colored coat.

"Going out?" she asked.

There was a certain tone of expectancy in her voice and she looked too intimately at him. It was these two things that made Finn move slowly closer towards the stairs.

"Yeah," he said blithely. "Going out."

Dovey took a step nearer to him, glancing briefly back into the apartment behind her.

"I'm taking Zach to Sunday school," she told him. "We could walk with you."

Finn's breath caught in his throat. He stammered awkwardly for a moment but before he could force a string of cohesive characters together, a young boy with the same wide, blue eyes as Dovey burst out of her apartment and clung to her legs.

"Mummy, Mummy," he called up at her, bouncing on his toes with sugary energy.

Dovey looked down at him crossly.

"Zachary, where are your manners?"

Zachary slowly glanced up at Finn, who gave the kid a wave hello.

"What do you say to Finn?" Dovey prodded her son.

Zachary sighed laboriously and reluctantly turned to Finn.

"Good morning," he mumbled.

A genuine smile lifted up the corners of Finn's mouth.

"Morning, Zachary," he said.

Dovey looked satisfied and patted her son's head.

The spotlight off of him, Zachary looked back up at his mother and tugged at her sleeve.

"I can't find my book bag," he told her.

Dovey's sunshine smile didn't falter.

"Did you check under your bed?" she asked.

Zachary pulled her harder.

"It's not there!" he told her insistently, clearly annoyed with his mother's fractured attention.

Irritation fettered the light in Dovey's eyes and Finn leapt on it.

"Well, I've got to get going," he announced loudly, moving again towards to the stairwell.

The disappointment on Dovey's face dulled her features.

"Oh, okay," she said. "Maybe we'll see you later?"

Finn smiled tightly at her and nodded.

"Yeah," he said. "See you later."

His foot hit the first step and he turned away from her. Dovey craned her neck to watch him until he disappeared, then let her son pull her back inside the apartment.

Finn tread quickly down the stairs, pulling his jacket across his shoulders and shaking off his interaction with Dovey as he went.

Today was Sunday. The chill of a damp, arctic morning drenched his bones and the thinning mist clung to his wake like frothy, store-bought cobwebs. The street had just begun to come alive and he dodged a frost-lacquered car as he crossed the narrow road. Footsteps echoed in eerie rhythm on the cold stone sidewalk and voices carried like blown whispers, strange as their owners were just dark shadows in the distance of the fog.

Finn had lost sight of her but he knew, this being the first day of a new week, where she would ultimately draw her destination, as she had on every Sunday since the day he had first come upon her, quite by accident, all those months ago. Surely it was years by now.

The park was not far from their building, planted in the shadow of towering apartment blocks and office buildings that loomed over it on all sides. When he had happened upon it he felt as though he had discovered a secret paradise, like a flower that had pushed its delicate nose up through a casket lid of concrete. Shaded by knotty oaks, a moss blanketed lawn coiled about a stone-framed pond where geese and ducks and the occasional snowy swan would paddle about the mirror-still surface, pinching the nibbles of stale bread thrown by children clinging to their mothers' legs. There were benches made of embossed iron and wood and one carved from a single, behemoth tree trunk. Children clamored over an ancient iron jungle gym, gales of laughter filling the air as parents and nannies kept watchful eyes.

The first time Finn saw her here she was sitting on a bench overlooking the pond, a slight, far sweeping wind rippling the water, the bustle of the playground behind her. A lone silky duck, plump beneath fawn-colored plumage, had been pecking at the frayed hem of her trousers, yet she was lost inside herself, her sallow face awash in shadow, the tempest gaze of her faraway eyes spellbound within the brackish water. He had thought he had seen a pearl of sorrow sliding down the lashed cusp of her eye but he couldn't be sure. Yet he knew she grieved some loathed suffering, recognizing as his own the venom of affliction in the tight, shivering clasp of her lips.

Every Sunday afterward he knew she was there, sometimes weeping, perhaps cursing some silent and wicked fate. This day would prove no exception as Finn spotted her sitting on her bench, the same one every time with the pond before her and the playground behind. She sat with her gloved hands folded tautly in her lap and her unlit gaze staring into emptiness.

She had dark eyes, Finn realized with a faint smile.

He left her there, as he always did, his heart heavier than when he arrived, unable to outstay the puzzling reason that kept her there. She would not return until nightfall. If only she knew that she was not as alone in this world as her woe besotted expression suggested. If only she knew someone waited up for her.

❦

The day trickled by with hateful sloth. The murmuring of his computer screen read 'November in Berlin.' He could no longer look at it and shut it off with tethered frustration. He knew what had happened that November in Berlin. It was the cause of his sleeplessness, yet he could not relive it today. He would try again tomorrow; he would be of stronger mind tomorrow.

Finn eyed the phone with bitter temptation but the well-worn slip of paper taped above it upon which he had scrawled Peter's number stung his tongue like poison and he thought better of it. He had already decided that forgiveness was sorely overrated. To pine in sightless aggression suited him best and fueled the heat of his silent revenge like breath on an ember. Rage stoked his penitence and spared him from wallowing in the blind pity of his own fallout.

The soft knock on his front door made him jump. He froze and remained completely still for a full minute, his eyes on the door. He was just exhaling with the relief of assuming whoever it was had decided not to persist when a second knock rapped against the door.

Finn got to his feet and crossed the apartment. He stuck one eye up to the peephole. Dovey stood on the other side, a patiently pleasant expression softening her delicate features, her vibrant, blue eyes sparkling.

Finn lowered his eyes, his hand hovering over the doorknob. A grimace of reluctance screwed up his face but he finally unlocked the door lock, smoothed his features, and pulled the door open.

Dovey's whole face seemed to light up. Her smile was blinding. Finn tried not to look away.

"Hi," she said.

"Hey, Dovey. What's up?"

"I just ordered Chinese food and there are mountains of extra," she told him. "Interested?"

Finn's body language stiffened. He glanced behind him into his quiet, empty apartment and turned back to her with a cringe of feigned disappointment.

"I can't," he told her. "I've got this article due and my editor is breathing down my neck to finish it. If I don't get it done tonight he's going to have my head."

Dejection made Dovey's bottom lip stick out. It was plump and glossy pink and made Finn eye her more closely. She'd reapplied her make-up before crossing the hall to knock on his door. Her hair was pinned back off her face, the soft pinky-red highlights in it glowing. She wore a dark blue shirt cut low to display the creamy swathe of her collar bones. A faint aroma of roses could be detected, growing stronger the longer she stood there on his doorstep. "Are you sure you can't sneak away for a bite?" she asked.

Finn shook his head.

"Afraid not." He made his voice hard, with not a trace of waver for her to hang on to.

"All right," she sighed. "But if you change your mind...."

"I know where you are," he said, smiling kindly.

Dovey smiled back, a serene, sweet, utterly unflappable smile, and Finn quickly moved back inside his apartment before that smile could grow on him.

"See you later," he said as he shut the door on her.

He waited there silently until he heard the faint patter of Dovey's retreat and the click of her front door closing. He turned around and scanned the quiet, dark spaces of his own home. It was strange. The light that he could see from Dovey's apartment on the occasions when her door was open was always bright and crisp and vivid. His was flat and dull, like a Communist's color palate. Maybe it was the light bulb wattage.

Another knock sounded against his front door, but this one was different; short, sharp raps from young knuckles. He opened the door and found Dovey's son standing before him with a plate piled high with Chinese food, coated in a hot cloud of steam vapor.

"Mummy said you were busy working so I should take this to you," he said a little nervously, like an unrehearsed actor trying to remember his lines.

The chilled shell of Finn's façade cracked and warmth spread out across his features, melting the aloof reservation he wore for Dovey. He bent down to the kid's eye level and took the plate from him.

"Thank you, Zach," he said.

Zachary smiled shyly and looked at his feet.

"You're welcome," he mumbled.

Then he seemed to remember something and dug into his pocket, handing Finn a plastic wrapped fortune cookie.

"Mummy said this one was yours because it was pointing towards your house," he said.

"Thanks," Finn murmured, charmed by the boys awkward mannerisms. "And thank your mother for me."

Zachary nodded and Finn watched him scamper back across the hall and disappear into his apartment. Finn caught a glimpse of strawberry blond hair before the door closed.

Finn sat the plate down on his kitchen counter, pulled a fork from one of the drawers, and ate standing up. He ate until the plate was clean, then cracked open the fortune cookie, popping shards of it into his mouth as he unrolled the fortune.

You will benefit from an act of generosity, it read.

"Well, duh," he murmured, scrunching up the fortune in his hand and tossing it in the garbage.

He stared at the empty plate. Now he would have to return it. Frustration muddled his expression and he rubbed his weary eyes. He glanced up at his ceiling. Still quiet. He pulled one of the kitchen stools over to him and sat down. Then he waited.

She returned at dusk. He heard the frail patter of her steps on his ceiling, a comfort like chocolate or that extra deadbolt on the door. Yet her return was strange and tied a knot of foreboding in

Finn's heart. Some odd unfamiliarity had followed her home and he was inexplicably troubled. She was pacing, furiously, like she would wear a dent into the floorboards. He was suddenly worried, and for the first time since she became to him what sound is to songbirds, he truly wished he knew her name to call her by it.

Then, as abruptly as it had sparked, her pacing stopped and the torture of stillness was what remained, like the eerie calm in the eye of a hurricane.

Finn despised these silences, as though she did it on purpose to torment him. He strained his ears and listened for the slightest of sound and there came none for the longest time until darkness had descended once again to envelope them. But on this night, this eve of some long wounded fear, Finn felt as though it were only he in all the world still waking.

He had decided around midnight to venture into writing by hand. A crisp, new notebook and a fine pointed pen clutched in his hands. Finn settled into a large, butter soft armchair. On the center of the first line he quickly wrote, 'November in Berlin.'

He waited, staring at the words until they bled into a single inky streak and his head began to brim with fog. The pen hovered off his fingertips over the page, the ink on the single strand of letters long dry and beginning to take the shape of some foreign language. He underlined them and leaned back to admire the pain of his craft, grimly satisfied.

The appeasement of this moment faded off his face like melting wax and was replaced by a hollow, long starved yearning.

"What are you doing?" he whispered bitterly.

A fat bauble of wet crimson suddenly dropped onto the page, like a clotted raindrop, and Finn furrowed his brow at it in silted bewilderment. When a second droplet landed beside the first, he brushed his fingertip across them, smearing the scarlet globules into a gauzy trench. He smelt vinegary iron that stung the back of his throat and, with dread, lifted his eyes to look above him.

A dark red shadow had stained the edge of his ceiling and a drenched streak snaked over his chair and pooled above him, a sagging depression shedding tears of blood. Slipping from the path of a ruby droplet, Finn balked to his feet, the pen and paper tumbling off his lap, the whites of his eyes staggered on the murky stain splaying the corner of his ceiling. His heart ballooned into his throat and choked the breath in his lungs, filling the insides of his veins with ice. He filched a newspaper from the magazine rack beside the chair and laid it over the seat, catching crimson raindrops with a pallid rhythm as they landed and spattered.

Finn slowly backed away, his mind shrieking horrors that severed his tongue. His wild stare still clinging to it, he crossed to the door, reaching for the brass polished knob with a hand that faintly trembled. The hall was silent as a tomb and the door echoed as he closed it on his back, causing his corseted nerves to flinch. The hush of his feet on the stairs was hollow to the raging of his heart as he rounded the stairwell and stopped on the landing. A sliver of light beneath her door cast a square of sheen across the floor. On the tips of his toes he neared it and pressed an ear to the door, wincing as the floor boards creaked beneath him.

Not a sound emanated from the flat, no brash at all, like it was empty, and Finn hesitated, sinking a deep breath into his belly before he rapped his knuckles across the door. His heart was drumming echoes in his ears as he waited for an answer that wouldn't come. He eyed the doorknob, identical to his own, and was besotted by a fear that quarreled with his nerve. But she was in there, of that he could be certain, and he swallowed his loathe and decided.

"What the hell," he whispered.

He grabbed the knob and turned and was taken aback with startle when the door swung wide.

Finn froze to the threshold as the door clanged against the wall and her flat lay before him, as alien as it was exactly as his own: a single, vast loft room, the far wall almost completely encased in glass, multi-paned like the bars of a cage. The door opened to a tiny kitchen nook and the walls beyond were stark white and unadorned. There was but a lone piece of furniture, an antique style iron-framed bed in one corner beside the windows, tucked beneath a patchwork quilt that looked homemade. A delicate lamp hung above it, burnished through panes of rainbow glass, lighting gauzy, candy-colored shadows over the flat.

Finn numbly realized that the bed stood over the plot of his red weeping ceiling and hot fear stole his breath. He took great, wooden strides to cross the flat, the rove of his stare catching a puddle of shiny crimson unfurling across the floorboards from beneath the bed.

Awareness ebbed as he found that he looked over the scene from somewhere beyond himself and his stride broke into a hastened bolt across the floor. His feet slipped in the sticky glaze of wet scarlet as he pushed the heavy bed away and dropped to his knees, congealed blood soaking through to his skin.

She was lying there as though she had fallen onto the crook of the floor between the wall and her bed, both wrists carved with deep, weeping slashes. A blood-caked pruning knife hung off her limp, red-smeared fingertips and her face was pale as death; her eyes shut. She appeared so serene that were it not for the sickly shade of her cast, she could be sleeping.

Finn's mind was blank as he leaned over her and pressed his ear against her chest, streaked with spears of parched scarlet like burnt ink. He could hear a heartbeat, frailer than a whisper, struggling against the cage of her ribs. He darted back onto his feet and searched desperately for a phone he couldn't find.

Finn stepped outside of himself and watched from a distance as he flung himself out the door, slipping down the stairs and stumbling back into his flat. He spattered his phone with her blood as he knocked it off its hook and plastered it to his ear. Time slivered by in agony and he couldn't hear himself as he spilled her distress to the faint voice on the other end. He tripped flying back up the stairs and was kneeling at her side before he even remembered he had left her. He tore the quilt down across her, pressing the fabric over her festered arms, snuffing the blood that spooled from the violent wounds.

Finn couldn't think, was numb with her still warm blood all

over him, feeling the pulse of her life waning against his palms. He stared into the lifeless pale of her face and willed her to open her eyes, terrified to look away, should he miss the cull of her last breath. He didn't realize that time had passed at all until a pair of dark clad paramedics were pulling him back. He couldn't feel his feet as he followed them down the perilous flights of stairs, her lithe body strapped into the gurney as though she would attempt an escape. The white tourniquets hastily wound around her wrists were already stained with faint dapples of scarlet.

When they slid her into the back of the ambulance, Finn didn't realize he held her limp hand in his, until the doors slammed shut behind them and the vehicle roared shrieking into the street.

Chapter Three

Finn sat in the waiting room, empty and alone in the hush of early morning. It was so quiet he feared to move and make a noise, would it distress the calm.

They had swept her away in a flurry, sticking tubes into her flesh and down her throat, pumping her chest with their hands clenched together. A nurse had given him paperwork to fill out and he did it only to push the image of her lifeless and bloody visage to the back of his head. Like porcelain she was so white and cold through the folds of her begrimed clothing. She could die without him ever knowing her name or the color of her eyes. Was it to be so, he would never forgive himself, for it wouldn't be her death that proved the truest tragedy. The sorrow of her leaving would pale in the absence of kind voices compiled to say goodbye.

He was startled when he felt the warmth of early sunshine cascading in through the sliding glass entrance doors. He had forgotten the time and didn't search out a cloak, but he did raise his weathered stare from the clasp of his white knuckled fingers to see a weary eyed doctor striding towards him, clip board in hand.

The doctor took a seat beside him and held Finn's bleary gaze. "She'll live," he said.

A wave of hot relief rolled off Finn's shoulders and the next breath he took felt like the first he inhaled since she had wept through his ceiling.

The doctor let it sink in a moment before he continued.

"We've sown and bandaged her wounds and she lost a lot of blood," he said.

"How many times," Finn suddenly found himself asking. "How many times did she cut herself?"

The doctor hesitated, quickly gauging Finn's mettle.

"Seventeen times," he finally said, watching Finn closely as the blood drained out of his features. "Six cuts on her right wrist, eleven on her left."

Finn felt a sick chill crawling up his throat and he took a deep breath to cork the back of his mouth. What abhorrent torment would drive someone to mutilate themselves so? What pain was so overwhelming that it suffocated life of all its tender hope? What kind of internal affliction could manifest itself in the slashing of one's own flesh by their own hand?

"It's lucky you found her when you did," the doctor said, breaking into his daze. "Another half hour or so she would be dead. I see here you wrote her name as R. LaMotte. You don't know anything else about her?"

"She lives above me," Finn told him, his voice numbed, the gape of his stare fixed on nothing.

"Yet you've listed yourself as her emergency contact?"

"I don't think she has anyone else," Finn answered absently, his mind faraway, in the smell of her blood drying against his skin.

The doctor was quiet a moment, watching the worriment furrowing Finn's face, the way his hands were shut so tightly together they shivered.

"She's awake."

It startled Finn and he turned up his eyes in damp surprise.

"She's been asking after you."

"After me?"

"The one who was holding her hand in the ambulance," the

doctor said. "Would you like to see her?" He motioned to a nurse standing nearby. "Nurse Archer can show you to her room."

Finn was staggered to find that that petrified him more than facing the loneliness of forever alone. For two years she had haunted the corners of everyday. For two years she had been a ghost, his ghost. It surprised him to realize she was real after all. It surprised him that he wasn't the only person who could see her.

He rose shakily to his feet, suddenly nervous.

"I don't... I don't think I can right now," he stammered. "I, um, have things to get back to. It's late anyway. I'll come back during regular visiting hours." He realized he was rambling and forced himself to stop.

The doctor and nurse shared a mildly surprised look, but had no emotional investment with which to persuade him. Finn himself looked confused as to why he was refusing. He gave the doctor an awkward thank you and fled for the exit as if someone was going to try to stop him.

The cold night air hit him in the face like a splash of ice water. He stopped as it knocked the wind out of him.

There, in the dawn hours of the morning and the yellow glare of the lights from the hospital behind him, Finn felt the frenetic pull of the different isolations; that of true solitude and that of being secluded in a society so saturated with like-minded lonely souls as to be screaming in a crowd and having no one turn their heads. Finn closed his eyes and sighed heavily, dismally, and it sounded like he'd scraped that breath from the dried-up bottom of himself, from the empty well, and it ached his entire being, bones and tendons and flesh and all, to expel it. His hot breath met the cold air in a vaporous cloud and stuck to his five o-clock shadow, forming tiny ice crystals around his mouth.

He opened his eyes.

The city had burnt the belly of the sky into a flaxen colored haze. No stars, no moon in the night anymore. How could anyone stare up into the scarred umbrella of a golden midnight and not feel disconnected? Finn couldn't name his loneliness but he could feel it. He lost more and more of himself every day he didn't name it. There was little left now. He looked down at his hand and flexed his blood smeared fingers, as if the now dry matter stung his skin. Her blood was in the creases of his fingerprints and the permanently etched lines on his palm, corporeal proof that he had touched her. He brought his hand up to his mouth and breathed into his cupped palm, moistening the dried blood. He kneaded it with his thumb until the red lines made flaky, gummy smudges then disappeared altogether.

Finn stared at his palm. A pink stain still remained, like spilt red wine on a white lace tablecloth. He rubbed his hand on his pant leg but he could still see the faint threads where her blood had originally dried, just a shade darker than his natural skin tone. It was like he was carrying her with him, like she was underneath his skin. He could shower and shave and wear a suit and tie and she'd still be there. She was permanent, a tattoo he would wear upon his soul for the rest of his life.

Finn took a short, deep breath, stuck his hands into his pockets, and walked back inside the hospital. He scanned the waiting room until he found Nurse Archer and slowly approached her. He was quiet until she looked up from her clipboard and acknowledged him.

"I'm back," he said sheepishly.

Her bed was next to a window, bright with the glow of a clear, cloudless dawn, and behind a thick, white curtain made from what looked like worn plastic. Everything stank of chemical cleanliness and Finn's feet echoed on the linoleum, polished to a reflective gleam, as he followed Nurse Archer. She stopped before the curtain and left him standing there.

Everything would change. He could feel it deeper than his bones. He had been feeling its portentous approach for many restless nights passed and he feared it would stay his leave long enough for the past he had abandoned to find him again. He was afraid, but he continued.

Her face was turned away towards the window when he crossed

the waxy barricade. He stood silent at the edge of her bed until she slowly drew back to look at him. Her face was warm, a pale blush of rose back in place across the parched chisel of her lips and cheekbones. She looked frail, her throat taut with stress, yet her mouth was painted with mirth ever so faint and the vast nets of her eyes were not surprised by his shadow, almost as though she had expected him. Her eyes were a glittering, golden brown.

All at once, Finn had so much to say and yet couldn't speak, blinded by the reality of her nearness and the sudden, closer, frailty of mortality, like acid on his tongue.

"Why don't you ask me," she said. Her voice crackled with thirst.

Finn slowly sat in the stiff, plastic chair beside the bed and looked at her wrists, bound in thick, white gauze like precious, breakable packages.

"Why would you do that?" he asked. His voice was a dry and arid husk and he had to clear his throat and repeat the question.

"Is that all you have to ask me?" she murmured softly.

Finn didn't hesitate.

"What is your name?" he said.

"Roxanne," she told him. "What's yours?"

"Finn," he said. "Why did you do that?"

"Is Finn short for something?"

Finn hesitated at her diversion, but when he saw the desperate pleading in her gilded eyes, he felt her fear in the deep of him like it had always been there and he only now was realizing it.

"Yeah," he said slowly. "Finnean. But no one ever calls me that."

"Why not?"

He smiled at her and felt warm as the chill of her eyes thawed.

"I don't know," he told her. "I guess they don't like the way it sounds when they say it."

Roxanne's face glazed with gentle wistfulness and she looked above her as though she could see a sun brilliant and warm through the sterile, water-stained ceiling of her room.

"I like it," she murmured. "Finnean... It sounds romantic."

Her face shadowed and the entire room seemed to dim as it did.

"Why did I do it," she breathed as though asking herself.

Roxanne sighed sadly, frail hurt rummaging the strings of her voice, and her stare went cold as ice against him.

"Why did it take me trying to kill myself for you to talk to me?" she asked, her lips pursed with soft amusement.

Finn's mouth would have dropped open was it not for the well-rehearsed timbre of her voice.

"So, this was for my benefit?"

"No," she answered quickly. "It was for mine. But I've seen you here and there. You never look anyone in the eyes. No. This didn't have anything to do with you. I am glad it's you who's here, though."

He felt he was sinking beneath the lightning of her gaze and had to look away before he lost himself there, pretending that frustration made him sever her tether on him and not the unsettling realization that her will even now was stronger than his own. She withdrew the painted serenity on her expression and agonized wonderment trembled her voice.

"I don't know why, Finnean."

Her voice was so small, a wispy hush, and for a timid moment Finn saw her with her mask undone and she was fragile as glass. She was fighting even now to stay afloat in this precarious haunt of life.

"You don't know why you wanted to die?" he asked even as he believed her, even as he understood her agony explicitly.

"I can't remember what it was I did yesterday that made me feel hopeless enough," she breathed, her voice faraway. "When I do, I'll let you know."

Roxanne's bewildered stare wandered into nothingness, her brow furrowed with perdition.

"I do not think I am supposed to be here," she said faintly.

Finn could feel the burden of her precocious heaviness drawing him nearer, like a moth to flame.

"Like my time ended a long time ago but for some reason I'm still here," she whispered, her eyes narrowed as she sorted out the syrupy webs behind her mind.

Her lissome gaze trawled back on him.

"Sometimes I think I'm a ghost," she told him, a smile painted on her mouth even as devastation writhed behind her eyes. "No one can see me unless I want them to, and even then, I'm more of an irritant than a revelation."

"I see you," Finn said with a deep soaked breath. "And I don't find you irritating."

"I know."

He didn't breathe as Roxanne held his stare like it wasn't his own, until the clatter of metal instruments from somewhere afar severed his attention.

"Is there anything you need?" he asked. "Anyone I can call for you?"

Her eyes darkened and she returned them to the window, shaking her head no.

"No one?"

"I just want to sleep," Roxanne told him, her voice abruptly brittle and acerbic.

Finn slowly nodded, the room suddenly cold as ice, and rose to his feet.

"I don't know if you should be left alone," he said, conflict stinging his tongue.

"I'm not," she breathed. "Can't you see them?"

She slowly turned to the confusion in his stare and a frail smile, genuine and beautiful as it was sad, purled over her lips.

"My demons."

Chapter Four

The place Finn returned to was very different from the place he had left. It was harsher, crueler, and cold. The beauty he could find in this world he called home was altered. It was somehow ugly now, like a dapple of rot on the blush of a ripe apple. It left a sourness on his tongue that stung his eyes.

Like roots had sprouted from his toes, Finn stood in his open doorway as pale sunlight cast strange gossamer shadow puppets across the boards of his floor. A soft hand fell against his arm and he nearly leapt out of his skin. He turned around with a hand clutching his thrashing heart to find Dovey standing behind him wearing a white terrycloth bathrobe and matching fuzzy slippers on her bare feet. She looked tired and pale with no make-up on her face, like she'd been waiting up all night.

"Gosh, I'm sorry, Finn," she said. The early hour made her whisper.

"That's okay, Dovey," he said, mimicking her hushed tone. "It's like five a.m. What are you doing up?"

"I heard all this commotion a few hours ago," she said. "Paramedics were rushing a woman downstairs. Did I see you with them?"

"Yeah, that was me. I've just come back from the hospital."

Dovey's body language became chilly. She crossed her arms over her chest and seemed to debate what she wanted to ask him next.

"Who is she?"

"Our upstairs neighbor," Finn told her.

Dovey looked at him blankly.

"Yeah, I don't really know her either," he murmured.

She warmed when he said that and a veil of concern needled her brow.

"Is she okay?"

Finn nodded brusquely with a short, weedy breath, glancing impatiently back inside his apartment as if he had some place to be.

"Yeah. It was just an accident," he said. "She's going to be fine."

Dovey laid her hand on his bicep and gazed up at him, her wide, blue eyes glittering like two tiny sapphire suns.

"Are *you* okay?" she asked.

Finn stared at her hand on his arm and his eyes slowly travelled up into her face. Her concern for him was genuine, so tangible it made the air around her dewy, even as it grew thorny with friction the closer to himself it became.

"I'm fine, Dovey," he said, very slowly pulling away from her hand.

Dovey's eyes dipped a little, then widened in grim surprise.

"Is that blood on your sleeve?" she asked timidly.

Color briefly splashed across the bridge of Finn's nose and he hid his arm behind his back.

"It's been a long night," he said wearily.

A kittenish smile curled up the corners of Dovey's soft lips.

"Well, if you ever need someone to talk to," she murmured, "Zachary's spending the weekend with my mother. Maybe we could go to dinner."

Finn couldn't look her in the eye.

"I think I'm going to be pretty busy the next little while," he said with difficulty. "I can't say I'm going to have any free time."

The sweetness in her expression soured only a little.

"Thanks, by the way," he said quickly, eager to salve the uncomfortable injury from her face, "for sending over the Chinese food yesterday. I have your plate."

He turned to retrieve the plate from his kitchen counter but Dovey grabbed his arm to stop him.

"There's no rush," she told him. "You can drop it by this weekend."

He opened his mouth to speak but she cut him off. Her hand on his arm softened.

"And before you say you're too busy, it only takes five minutes to return a plate."

He smiled half-heartedly.

"Then why don't I just give it to you now?" he asked.

Dovey's affectionate smile grew.

"Will you look at the time," she murmured. "I'd better go. Zachary will be waking up soon."

She squeezed his arm and held his gaze for just a second before turning and walking back to her apartment. For the first time, Finn watched her go.

After a moment, he shook his head, tried to rub the ache of sleep from his eyes, and returned to his apartment with even more heaviness than he had been carrying five minutes before. He stood in the middle of his home and hung his head in the quiet. There had never been a time in Finn's entire life where he felt more isolated. There was no patter on his ceiling anymore.

He was still for a very long time. When he did move again, time had eclipsed his mourning and he retrieved a mop and bucket and salved the crimson stain from the canopy of his ceiling. He trekked up the stairs, the door to her flat still hanging open in a wide yawn, and washed the inky puddle from her floor. He plucked the caked knife between two fingers and held it out far from himself, dropping it into the empty sink and letting water course across it until its gilt edge was clean.

He left it there.

Finn didn't linger long. The room felt uninviting without her footsteps in his head, as though it had a heartbeat and didn't want him there. When he returned to his flat it was with an emptiness he did not expect and he quickly found that he missed her, like a friend.

A blush of rose red was imprinted on his ceiling, faint like a gauzy shadow, and he moved the chair that sat beneath it to the other side of the flat. Instead, he pushed his bed in its place so that when she dreamed, it would be from above him.

Finn sat like a stone in front of his computer and attempted to work. The screen was blank and try as he might to bring the words in his head to the words at his fingertips, there was nothing there. Only her face, pale and life bled. Only her blood, still weeping, unraveling in his hands, only her.

He pushed away from his desk and listed back in his chair, his eyes wandering the hollows of his flat, like the echoes in a cavern. He waited only a moment before he left again.

The streets were empty and shone with gossamer mist and nary a vehicle passed him as he walked. He went with no set direction in his head but found with little surprise that he had carved a footpath back to the hospital.

He walked the emptied corridors, all still and hushed around him like the gallows of the city library. A quiet that was strict and expected, that made one want to whisper their whispers.

Finn watched her through the open door of her room. She was asleep, her eyes shut. Her chest rose and fell to a gentle rhythm that comforted him, though he couldn't tell if it was a natural or medicated slumber. She seemed peaceful to him, in the peace that only sleep can harbor, and he envied her that, to be able to leave the world behind and shape the grand adventures that were only hers when she dreamed. Then again, perhaps they were medicated. Perhaps any kind of peace at all existed now only in one's memory of a time when they felt it, if they ever really did. Perhaps peace was the unattainable happy family of his generation, always in mind and never within reach.

Roxanne.

Roxanne LaMotte.

It did not seem she could be real with a name, so long had she been just a face.

Roxanne LaMotte.

She was still such a secret and he yearned to understand what it was that made her, that provoked her, that stirred and stayed her, what made her weep and laugh.

But for now he left her sleeping and when at last he found himself home, he laid his head upon his pillow, thought of her dreaming, and, just as the rest of the city was waking, fell asleep.

Chapter Five

By the time Finn woke, the sun was cresting the roof of the sky and on its way back down again. A thin skin of smog and cloud covered the orb, making it look anemic, a pale palomino moon at midday. He turned over onto his back and stared at the ceiling as he inhaled a great yawn and stretched his taut arms over his head. He'd fallen asleep on top of his covers and in his clothes. He peeled off the stale articles and stumbled into the shower. The water rinsed away the bloodstains on his hands and underneath his fingernails and washed his body clean.

But, as he wiped wet steam from the mirror, he looked anything but refreshed. He looked at once defeated and restless. Water dripped down his arms, over a connect-the-dots of tiny, pinprick-like scars. His fingers chattered anxiously against the edge of the sink. He opened the medicine cabinet and picked up every pill bottle and shook them, movements that were unconscious, rehearsed, like he'd acted them out a thousand times before. Each bottle was empty and he placed them back on the little round impressions they'd made in the sticky dust. He eventually shut the cabinet without retrieving anything and his hand came away squeezed into a tight, shaking fist that distended the veins in his arm.

Dressed, he walked into the kitchen. He stared at the food in his fridge but none of it was appetizing. It wouldn't take food to slake the hunger fueling his anxiety.

It was the quiet that was bothering him most, the painful awareness that she was gone. But now she was aware of *him* and it seemed like she always had been. Finn's head began to spin. A dozen different, combative emotions were running through him all at once. Like water through his fingers, he couldn't grab a hold of any of them save one. He would admit only to himself that his interaction with her the night before had scared him.

It had also left him dissatisfied and he needed to know what happened to her. She was so beautiful to him, so untouchable, that it had been a shock to learn her own world view was so ugly, and so close to the ground all she saw was dirt. She was so much the only light in his dull, enervated life that it was impossible for him to think she saw any blackness at all. It seemed like it should be wrong. She should have been happy.

And yet, he had been watching her long enough to know very well that she was sad. It wasn't just because she was alone. He knew people could be alone and still perfectly happy. It had happened to him on occasion. It was her eyes, her dark eyes that began black and spiraled outwards into circles of gold. They had no warmth in them at all, just like he had never seen her honestly smile.

Finn should have known better than to expect her to be warm but that was still what he looked for in her, in her looking at him. He wanted her to be the mirage in his head because there she was, perhaps not happy, but at least not suicidal. He almost felt hurt that she would decide to leave him, even though they'd never spoken and she was mostly just a figment of his imagination. He wanted to go back to when she was perfect in his mind; flawed, yes, and more than most, but that only made her more luminous to him; that only made her stand out all the more clearly and brightly against a background of stodgy normalcy. And he felt guilt down to his marrow when he thought that, because even her ice cold stare had melted him.

Finn hadn't been so emotionally stimulated in years. It was making him dizzy, his skin humming like she had burned him, and he couldn't stand it. He wanted to tear his skin off just to make it stop. It was too much all at once but his body seemed bent on making up for all the years of numbness, when there had been nothing, and no one, that could reach him. Where his skin had once been hard as iron was thin as tissue paper now.

He was on the verge of pulling his hair out. The silence was too much. He could hear himself so clearly. He couldn't take it. He grabbed his jacket from its hook and rushed out the door. As he pulled his arms through the sleeves, he descended the stairs two at a time.

It had never bothered Finn that the building didn't have an elevator. He liked the way climbing up and down the stairs made his heart race. It was just about the only stimulation the tired, scarred muscle got anymore and he was out of breath by the time he reached the sidewalk. The air was heavy and rich with the city, with only the palest nettles of winter stinging his exposed skin. There he stopped, glancing left then right in the two directions he could take. One would lead him to the hospital. The other would lead him backwards. He looked longingly left, and for a very long time, before turning right.

He walked with his head down, his eyes skirting anxiously back and forth. He knew what he was looking for and he wouldn't find it here with the little cafés, and boho boutiques, and private security guards who chased all the homeless people away. He kept walking.

After almost an hour, he passed a middle school, one of the more prosperous facilities where the students wore blazers and were driven around in Escalades. School was still in session and Finn walked a little further. A block away was a small park with an unkempt basketball and tennis court. There were few people in the park but one man was sitting on a bench outside the court reading a newspaper, or pretending to. Finn walked up to him and the man on the bench looked up from his paper as he approached, squinting good humouredly into the slate grey wall of sky behind Finn's head.

"What do you need?" he asked.

Finn set his jaw hard, the muscles popping. He shoved his hands into his pockets and cleared his throat.

"What've you got?" he said. He spoke through his teeth and stared back at the man on the bench as if forcing himself not to look away. It wasn't easy. His skin was crawling just being there. His heartbeat was thunderous, pounding blood and adrenalin in his ears.

The man looked him up and down and had him sized up by the time his wolfish eyes returned to Finn's head.

"How long's it been?" he asked.

Finn's hands in his pockets clenched into fists.

"What've you got?" he said again.

The man smiled up at him, an oily, predatory smile that dug beneath Finn's skin and scraped bone.

"I've got what you need," he said.

Finn fingered the folded bills in his pocket and looked more closely at the dealer. The suit he wore didn't fit him right. The gold watch on his wrist was a fake. The newspaper was yesterday's, a leave behind he probably just found on the bench. His shoes were scuffed and worn beneath a thick veneer of black shoe polish. Everything about him was for brief, grab-and-go encounters, and pain abruptly wormed its way into Finn's expression. It was all so terribly familiar. He'd been exactly there before. People just like this had once held so much power over him. The only substitute was the body in the suit.

It was startling how easy it was to slip backwards, so much easier than moving on... so simple, not yet painful. Finn felt like he'd been slapped in the face. There was something else that was missing; the sick, overwhelming excitement.

Finn retracted his hand from his pocket. It was empty. He backed up a few feet before turning away. He passed a shivering, rail thin blond with runny mascara heading towards the man on the bench as he left the park and kept walking.

The nurse circled Roxanne's bed, checked the IV, and left her sleeping. As soon as the nurse was gone, Roxanne's eyes fluttered open and she sat up. For several minutes she didn't move, her eyes on the open doorway to the hall, then she began tugging at the bandage around her left wrist. She pried at it until the soft, cottony material loosened and she was able to slowly unwind it. She was very careful when she neared the stitches. Some of the gauze was sticking to her dried wounds and she peeled it away like pulling off a layer of her own skin.

Roxanne's wrist was swollen and enflamed. The sown cuts were angry red and pushed against the wiry, black stitches like bread baking around string. She ran her hand over the crusty ridges and winced at the sting.

From the corner of her eye she caught movement by the door and collapsed back beneath the covers like all the air in her body had deflated. She shut her eyes tight and pretended to be sleeping.

She heard the sounds of someone tiptoeing to her bedside and pausing, as whoever it was checked to see if she was really asleep. After a moment, they sat something down on the small, rolling table beside her bed and footsteps began fading back towards the door. Roxanne's eyes fluttered open an inch, just enough to make out the retreating figure between her feathery eyelashes. Her eyes sprang wide and she bolted upright.

"Finn!"

Finn stopped with a start and whirled around as a great, uninhibited grin spread across her mouth. Her smile dazed him for a moment and it took him a few seconds to recover his voice.

"I thought you were sleeping," he said as he made his way back to her.

She shook her head as she sat back against her pillow and smoothed out the rumpled sheets over her lap. She kept her left wrist hidden underneath the blankets.

Her smile was luminous and Finn found himself watching her mouth, the delicate corners curling upwards, the sheen of saliva on her pillowy lower lip, the pearly white of her large front teeth.

"No, I wasn't sleeping," she told him. "You came back. I didn't think I'd see you again. What are you doing here?"

Finn frowned as he pulled a chair over to her bedside.

"You didn't think you'd see me again?" he asked. "What, you mean ever?"

Roxanne shrugged.

"I don't make a good first impression," she said.

The way she said it, the tone of her voice, almost suggested that she was painfully aware of the way Finn felt about her, of what he had thought after their official introduction. It unnerved him and he lowered his eyes as they clouded over. But Roxanne only smiled warmly and leaned her head to the side to try and catch his gaze again.

"What are you doing here?" she asked again.

Finn's expression brightened. He reached up and grabbed the paper grocery bag he had placed on the rolling table top.

"Well, I figured you wouldn't find hospital food very sustaining," he said.

He pulled out several items and Roxanne's eyes grew wide.

"Fresh fruit salad and French bread baked this morning," he said, placing the food stuffs on the table beside her.

Her eyes followed them, an almost astonished gape on her face. Finn grinned excitedly at the brightness her irises adopted and she slowly glanced away from what he had brought her and met his stare.

"How did you know?" she asked. Her eyes were almost glittering. "Those are from my favorite bistro downtown. I eat that salad every day... How did you know?"

Finn shrugged.

"Lucky guess," he said.

Roxanne smiled again and it was weightless. It seemed so strange, under these circumstances, in these surroundings, that she could smile like that at him. Finn procured two forks and they dug into the fruit salad together. She watched him out of the corner of her eye as she speared a grape and held it up to her mouth, stopping just before biting into it.

"Do you have a girlfriend?" she asked.

He glanced up at her in surprise.

"What?"

She didn't ask him again. They both knew he had heard her. Her smile just became a little more supple.

"No," he said after a moment.

"Why not?"

Finn gave her a self-deprecating smile.

"I'm not an adventurous individual," he said, "at least not anymore."

"What about Dovey Charles?"

His expression dimmed and he frowned.

"How do you know Dovey Charles?" he asked. "And how do you know to use her in that context?"

Her expression became demure.

"A woman knows," she told him expressively. "And I know the names of everyone in the building."

"Really? That's like two dozen people."

She nodded.

"Twenty-three people actually."

He eyed her skeptically.

"What about that old European guy whose newspapers you recycle for him?"

"John Vladimir."

"Okay. Who's that old cat lady one floor below me?"

"Hazel Barton."

"What about—"

"Belle Prescott, and her Dalmatian's name is Hugo."

A completely charmed smile stretched across Finn's mouth.

"You didn't even know what I was going to say."

She smiled back at him.

"Didn't I?"

They stared at one another until the smiles faded.

"So, how long are you going to be here?" he asked.

Roxanne looked down at the bowl of fruit salad. She speared a cube of bright orange mango and popped it into her mouth.

"They want to keep me here for observation," she said after swallowing. "Which, I suppose, is a polite way of telling me they think I'll try to hurt myself again."

"You wouldn't, would you?"

She looked up at him.

"Do you know me well enough to ask me that?"

He held her gaze and shook his head. The brief energy of friction between them made his heart flicker.

"No," he said, "I guess I don't."

Roxanne's eyes sank back down to her lap. She sighed discontentedly and distress pierced Finn's expression. He watched her from beneath the shade of his eyelashes. She seemed to be deliberating something.

Finally, she sighed again and raised her left arm above the covers, showing him the criss-cross of angry red slashes and purpling bruises against her milk white skin, the black tails of each knotted stitch sticking up like tiny porcupine quills. Finn's first instinct was to look away. It was truly horrible but that wasn't why. These wounds just seemed like such an intimate, personal thing.

"They've sent this psychiatrist to see me," Roxanne murmured. Her own eyes traced the bruised, scabbing trenches in her flash, like paper cuts magnified tenfold. "I don't like him. He talks to me like I'm going to blow away. I know what I did. He doesn't have the right to form an opinion of me. He just met me this morning. His cologne makes my eyes water. I think he might try to keep me here."

"What will you do then?" Finn asked.

She shook her head.

"I don't know."

"Will you stay?"

"I don't know."

"Are you going to be okay?"

Inexplicably, Roxanne's eyes filled with tears. Her pale lips began to tremble and she pressed her fingers to them to stop it. She turned away towards the window and the dusky yellow light filtering in through the blinds and Finn watched a round, glass-like teardrop pool on the edge of her eyelashes and glide down the graceful profile of her cheek. He gazed at her with mounting fear, the color falling from his face.

"I don't know," she whispered against her fingertips.

The agony of helplessness knifed Finn's features. There was more pain in that one tear and in the silvery way in which she spoke, like her voice was dust, than there was in all of his scars combined. He was equally desperate and hopeless to help her and the fact that he wasn't sure if it was selfishness or selflessness that motivated this yearning, made it all the more unbearable.

"Roxanne, isn't there anyone I can call for you?" he asked.

A faintly sweet smile shone through the bitterness on her face.

"That's the first time you've said my name," she murmured.

Surprise dotted his eyes. This woman was twisting his head into a pretzel. She was at once intimate and aloof; affectionate and guarded; perfect and damaged beyond repair; light and darkness. Her exile was chosen but she was lonely. She was too beautiful to be alone other than by choice. He had seen other men look at her, at the park, passing her on the street. Did she not even see them or did she truly not know how beautiful she really was? Why had she never responded to a single glance or smile or door held open for her? Finn felt like she had chosen him and couldn't understand why; why color kissed her face when she looked at him; why her eyes glittered; why she smiled when he said her name for the first time. She was seeing something in him that he couldn't see himself.

"I'm glad you came today," Roxanne said. "Thank you for thinking of me, Finn."

Finn was well aware she had shirked his question about contacting anyone for her but he didn't care. A wide grin stretched across his mouth. His heart was rattling in his chest like ice cubes in a blender. He looked happy. He *felt* happy. *She* made him feel that way. With no visage of the fantasy, of the girl he stared at through the glass and all that she was that he had made up for her, she was real. She was blood and muscle and bone and so much more a complex creature than had ever been created. She had a mind of her own, and whim and desire and tempestuousness. A word from him could make her happy or angry and discovering these things that swayed her either way thrilled him. He liked her more this way. He liked her better as a product of the world, bruises, scrapes and damage and all, than as the dressed up product of his own head and loneliness. Her darkness made her light shine that much more brightly. Her pain made her smile that much more joyous when she revealed it. Her damaged heart made him all the more riveted.

He didn't know how, or even if he could, but he was going to help her, even if that meant just being there, and even if *that* meant he was really helping himself. He wasn't just enamored with the distraction. It was Roxanne. It really was her. She made his cold heart flutter.

"Of course I think of you, Roxanne," he told her. "Do you really not know the impression you've made on me?"

Roxanne looked down at her ravaged wrist.

"No, no," he said quickly. "It's not that. It's..." He stopped. He couldn't tell her. He didn't trust himself to make sense to her and he was afraid of scaring her. "It's not that. I don't think of what you did when I think of you at all." His brow furrowed. "Actually, it's a surprisingly minor detail."

A soft smile lit up her eyes.

"It is? I was afraid it would influence your opinion of me," she said.

He smiled at her.

"There's nothing that could do that," he said.

Roxanne grinned and looked down at her hands, folded placidly together.

"Don't say that," she murmured. "Now there's no place to go but down."

"I wouldn't judge you, Roxanne," he told her. "I have no right."

Her expression softened as she looked at him. The color in her cheeks seemed to shimmer, like a peach dusted with sugar.

"Thank you, Finnean," she said quietly.

Finn tried to shear the wide grin from his face but it was dastardly and stubborn and he only managed to shake it.

"You're welcome, Roxanne," he murmured.

She hesitated a moment, her teeth nipping the inside of her bottom lip, and looked up at him.

"Will you come back to see me?" she asked.

The uncertainty in her voice surprised her.

"Yes," he said. "I would like to very much."

She smiled again and it made his heart skip a beat.

"Maybe you'll bring me dinner," she said.

"Maybe I'll *take* you to dinner."

Her eyes lit up.

"Really?"

Her excitement was infectious. It made him laugh.

"Yeah," he said. "If you want to."

"Would it be a date?"

He nodded.

"Yeah," he told her.

Her enthusiasm dimmed a little.

"I'm not very good at those kinds of things," she said.

"That's okay. Neither am I really."

Her eyes filled with tears again and Finn's face fell.

"It's not possible," she said, her voice a haunted husk of want and sorrow. "I'd like that, Finn. I'd really like that. But I can't just go out to dinner like a normal person. I can't function in normalcy. I've tried to act like I know that I should but I just... I can't. I don't know why I can't just be like everyone else. I just can't pretend."

The friction of anguish was eating up the softness in her voice and Finn leaned forward with a hand raised to hush her.

"That's okay," he told her. "It's all right, Roxanne. You don't have to do anything you don't want to. I don't want to push you."

She shook her head and, with great difficulty, forced words onto her tongue, her eyes shut tight in concentration.

"It's not that," she said. "I want to. I just... can't." She opened her eyes. As she did, a glassy tear dropped away from her eyelashes and slid down her cheek. "I'm sorry I can't help you understand."

He shook his head, desperate to rid the distress from her face, to make her smile again, to make her glow like he had managed to do before. He wanted to erase this pain she was holding onto, or at least share it.

"That's okay," he said. "Really, please, Roxanne, don't cry. I didn't want to upset you."

Roxanne looked away, a hand pressed over her mouth, her face burning red. Tears tumbled over her fingers. Finn hung his head into his hands in disbelief that the air between them could turn so suddenly cold and that his pleading with her could be okay had no effect on her, seemed only to make her more miserable.

"Roxanne, it's okay," he told her. He had washed the anxiety from his voice and made it firm and gentle, like his tongue was wrapped in velvet. "You don't need to tell me anything about you," he said. "Who you are doesn't matter to me." He cringed at how that sounded in his head but didn't try to repair it. "I just want to be in your life."

Roxanne inhaled a jittery breath and looked at him. The tears in her eyes made her irises look like they were bleeding.

"Why?" she asked.

Finn stared at her. He had no answer for her. For several seconds he tried to hustle one together but every word he found sounded false somehow, like if *he* didn't believe it, how was he supposed to convince *her* of its validity? He let the panic to comfort her evaporate, then met her eyes again when it was gone.

"I don't know," he said. "Honestly? I don't know. I just know I feel like I want to be here for you. I want you to call me if you need me. I want you to need me." He smiled and reached into an inside pocket of his coat. He pulled out a pen and grabbed one of the napkins that had come with the food he brought. "I'll prove it," he said, and scribbled a number down on the napkin.

Roxanne watched his hand and the black tip of the pen as it moved across the coarse paper. Finn capped the pen and put it back in his pocket. He looked up and held out the napkin to her, the corners of his mouth curling upwards.

"This is my phone number," he told her. "I want you to call it, day or night, if you need me, even if it's just to talk."

Roxanne eyed the slip of paper in his hand. Her eyes danced between it and Finn's eager face and a very small smile shaped her mouth. She reached out and took the napkin. Without looking at the number, she folded the paper in half three times, then closed her fingers around it and slid her hand underneath the covers. The encouraging smile she gave him was only for his benefit.

"Thank you," she murmured.

"Promise me you'll use it if you need to," he said.

She nodded and the pleasure in her smile was genuine.

"I promise." She rolled her eyes, dissatisfied with herself. "God, you must think I'm a real piece of work."

"Definitely, but that's not a bad thing."

Her eyes dipped as her returning smile washed a faint pastel of color into her cheeks and Finn gazed at her affectionately.

"You won't understand this," he said, "but you saved me today. You gave me a place to go. I owe you."

Her brow furrowed in confusion but the smile didn't falter from her lips.

"I think we can just say we're even," she murmured.

Finn grinned and nodded his head. His smile faded just a little and his eyes became sad. He glanced back towards the hallway and noticed for the first time that the nurses were keeping a close eye on them.

"I should get going," he said. "I don't want to wear out my welcome."

Roxanne's disappointment was very subtle. He didn't catch it.

"I guess I should try to get some actual sleep," she said.

When Finn's eyes turned back towards her, they were stained with pain. It was old pain, long simmering within him, but fresh to the surface and as vivid as the bright red blood of an open wound.

"Look, could you do something for me?" he asked.

Perdition sheathed Roxanne's tongue but she gave him a faint nod to continue.

"Even if it's a lie," he said, "could you tell me you're going to be all right?"

Surprise stunned Roxanne's expression and for a moment it was a blank slate. She stared at him like a scientist examining an experiment and trying to decide if it had succeeded or not. But then her golden irises bleared and a tender visage of warmth enveloped her whole face. Finn's mouth hung open in wonderment. In the dying tethers of afternoon light, she seemed to glow and for a moment he couldn't tell if the light was coming through the window or from Roxanne herself.

"I'm going to be all right," she told him.

Finn couldn't tell if she was lying or not.

Chapter Six

When Finn arrived back home, out of breath from jogging up the stairs, he shrugged his coat from his shoulders and flung it aside. He sat down at his computer and began to type. 'November in Berlin' flew off his fingertips.

The last pale shards of daylight disappeared behind the horizon of the buildings across the street and dipped the apartment in darkness but Finn continued typing. Like a zombie, he stared at the computer screen and moved only to blink and strike the keys with his fingers, awash in a cocoon of electrical blue light.

Somewhere around three in the morning he fell asleep and awoke with a start when a car alarm from the street below began to shriek. Morning was sifting through his large front window and he could hear the myriad sounds of people leaving for the day; cars starting and grumbling as the engines warmed; a bus passing; a group of kids on their way to school, talking up a storm and seemingly unaware that in this early hour there was still some of the city trying to sleep; Belle Prescott and her Dalmatian, Hugo, on the sidewalk, the canine barking madly at a big, black standard poodle across the street.

Finn rubbed the sleep from his eyes and leaned back in his chair to stretch. His eyes refocused on the screen of his computer. He'd written twenty-seven pages.

He rose to his feet and walked into his small kitchen, filling his coffee maker and turning it on. He yawned heavily as coffee colored liquid began to trickle into the glass pot, and turned his eyes to his phone. If it rang, he looked like he wasn't sure if he would answer it.

Finn poured himself a large cup of coffee, left it black, and returned to his computer. The adrenalin from his time with Roxanne had faded and he was reluctant to continue. He closed his eyes and thought of her alone in her hospital bed. He wondered how her night had been and he could only imagine it as being miserable. He'd spent nights in hospitals before. Florescent lights; the constant din of faraway noise, like voices in the fog; the smell of sick and ammonia. He hadn't slept. It was impossible to sleep in that. How did anyone expect her to get better?

He wanted her to call him. He wanted her to need him. He outstayed the rest of the day waiting for her to use the number he had given her. Why? Maybe she was okay. Maybe she had told him the truth. He thought of her arms, her long, willowy arms, and her milk white skin that looked creamy as butter if he ran his hands over it. He didn't think of the cuts, or the scars that would form that she would wear for the rest of her life. He didn't think of the people who would stare at her, and at him if he was with her. He pulled up the sleeve of his shirt and looked at his own scars, the ones *he* would wear until he died. He thought of how many people he had let into his life since he had stopped adding to them and realized he had been alone for a very, very long time.

Finn looked up at the screen. He saw her there, too. He saw her choice in the choices he had made. He saw her isolation in his loneliness. He saw her death wish in the way he had once taken care of himself. He saw her wounds in his scars and felt the same pain they inflicted.

He turned back to the phone. He wanted her to call him. He wanted her to because he didn't want to be the only one falling.

Chapter Seven

Finn awoke to the ringing of his telephone. Still heavy with sleep and dreams that had already flown him, a voice now familiar met him when he picked up the receiver and put it to his ear.

"Finn?"

She was whispering, as though the world had ears.

"Roxanne? Roxanne, are you there?"

A chill silence baited her words.

"I need your help."

Worry frayed his voice.

"Are you all right?" he asked, rolling from his bed and striking the bare soles of his feet on the cold wood floor.

"You were right, Finn," she said. "I'm not okay on my own. They look at me like I'm crazy."

Her voice tripped and he heard her swallow a wretched sob.

"Yours is the first kind face I can remember," she told him, the wounds festering in her words deeper than the wounds in her flesh. "They want to keep me here."

Her words bled together in a sudden torrent of bitter grief and Finn's hands threaded into fists at the torturous battle of her fighting it.

"It's all right," he hushed. "It's going to be okay. Where are you?"

"I'm still in my room," Roxanne managed, her voice quivering. "They don't want to let me leave."

"They won't release you?"

"No."

Finn took a deep breath and found he didn't have to hesitate.

"Stay where you are," he told her. "I'm coming to get you."

Finn pulled up to the hospital doors and left his car, the dashboard of which was black with dust for his seldom use of it, in a no parking zone. He half speed-walked, half ran through the lobby to the elevator. His whole body was humming with nervous energy. As he waited for the metal doors to open, his foot bobbed anxiously up and down and his fingers tapped a messy rhythm against the wall. When he pushed his unruly mop of black hair off his forehead, it flopped back into his eyes like he was an inherently disheveled creature and there was nothing he could do to change that or present himself as if he was all together.

All the lights in Roxanne's room were ablaze as he approached it. When he entered he found Roxanne perched on the edge of her bed. She was wearing only a flimsy hospital gown and robe, the sleeves pushed up above her elbows, and her feet were bare. There was blood on her arm where she had pulled the needle of her IV from her vein. The blood had run down and stained the white sleeve of a fresh bandage wrapped around her wrist. She looked like she had been crying, her gaunt cheeks piebald with irritation, and when her stormy eyes fell upon him, she looked almost startled to see that he had come.

There was a nurse and a doctor in a sterile white lab coat sitting with her and when Finn entered the room, Roxanne stood to her feet and pointed him out to them.

"I told you," she said, clearly agitated, to the doctor.

The doctor looked surprised by Finn's appearance as well and slowly stood to his feet and approached him. Roxanne folded her arms across her chest and sat back down with a huff of irritation and an icy glance at the nurse.

"I'm Dr. Greenway," the doctor introduced.

He stuck out his hand to Finn.

"Finn," he said, shaking the doctor's offered hand. "I'm here to take her home."

The doctor's cologne made his eyes water.

Dr. Greenway sucked a sharp breath into his mouth.

"I'm very reluctant to release her," he said. "I believe Ms. LaMotte still is a danger to herself. I want to admit her into my clinic for further observation."

Finn felt himself turning greener with each word the doctor said to him. He could see why Roxanne would be adverse to his suggestion. He had a very clinical, impersonal manner of speaking, as if Finn was just a cardboard cutout. He stood very close, almost as if in an attempt to intimidate Finn. Finn's eyes only narrowed with resolve. He folded his arms across his chest and stood his ground, Roxanne's shape always in the blurry corner of his peripheral vision.

"You can release her into my care," he said.

Dr. Greenway blinked in surprise. He eyed Finn more closely, suspicious of this declaration.

"I don't think you understand what that would entail," he said. "She'd be your responsibility." He put extra emphasize on the word *'your.'*

Finn nodded impatiently.

"No offense, doctor, but this isn't the most healing of environments," he said. "You're just making her scared keeping her here. She'll get better once I take her home."

"You can't know that. *I*, on the other hand—"

Finn cut the end of his sentence off.

"Look, I know you mean well and you're just trying to do your job, but I'm not leaving without her. So, you and I could argue about this for however long it takes you to feel like you've gotten your point across, or you can give me the paperwork now and we'll be out of your hair in ten minutes."

Without waiting for the doctor's reply, and looking slightly dazed by his own forcefulness, Finn walked around him to Roxanne, who stood to her feet as he approached. He took off his coat and draped it over her shoulders and began guiding her to the door.

Ten minutes later, he was helping her into the passenger side seat of his car.

Neither spoke as they left the hospital behind them and melted into a light current of traffic. Dusk was swiftly leaving them when they reached their building and Finn rushed Roxanne inside as though time was somehow against them. He hurried her up each flight of stairs until they reached the threshold of her flat and everything slowed. Roxanne halted before her door, Finn silent at her back, watching her intently as she stared at the brassy doorknob as though she half expected herself to be behind it, to open the door and meet herself.

Nothing met her when at last she stole a breath into her lungs and pushed the door open. The flat was dark and still, just as Finn had left it; cold and bereft without her.

Roxanne slowly crossed into the room, her bare feet lapping over the hard-wood floor like the patter of a child trying to be silent in the earliest hour of morning. Finn was frozen in the doorway, his eyes filled with her, as she investigated this place that was no longer hers alone.

"Did you want anything?" she asked, her voice hollow, like it wasn't hers, as she stopped for a moment, her body half turned towards him.

"Do you *have* anything?" he asked, leaning slightly inside.

"I could offer you coffee but I can't get to the spoons to stir it," she said, her voice inexplicably swallowed by a deep hopelessness. "The drawer's stuck."

Finn's eyes wandered to the kitchen counter, finding a drawer that looked as though some beast had raked its claws across the wooden face.

"You know, you can buy spoons," he said slowly.

Her sharp shoulders slumped.

"But I don't need spoons," she sighed. "I *have* spoons. I just can't get to them."

Her voice fell away when she saw that the bloody pool by her bed had been salved away and she turned back to him, her eyes glittering in the dim light.

"Did you..."

Finn only nodded.

"That's what you never think about," Roxanne whispered as she neared the vast, empty window, "what happens when your soul flies away but your body stays behind. There will be someone who will find you. It could be a loved one. The numbness is just so potent. It doesn't let you ponder what will be without you."

She raised a hand and laid her palm flat against the chill of the glass, the hatchling of a frail sunset in the distance.

"Each morning born anew," she breathed as if to herself, or to whom she was, who she had left behind.

Finn felt suddenly invisible and turned to leave. Her voice caught him and didn't want to let him go.

"Please don't go."

He turned back around, frozen in her doorway. Her back was to him and for a pale moment he believed she had spoken to her own reflection in the window.

"Please don't leave."

She looked back at him and there was desperation in the wallows of her eyes. He wavered a minute and closed the door, sealing them inside the flat. He wanted to stand beside her but halted short of reaching her, shoving his hands into his pockets and waiting for her, as there was so much that was hanging above her head.

"Do you have regrets?"

Her voice startled him, stronger than he had expected.

"What?"

"If you died today, would you have regrets?" she murmured. "Things you did. Things you didn't do."

Finn didn't have to think.

"Yes."

Roxanne shook her head.

"Why do we do this?" she wondered hazily. "Why are we bent on destroying ourselves? Why are we so afraid...."

"What are you afraid of?" Finn asked.

Roxanne leaned against her shoulder and listed her brow on the glass as he slowly ventured into the threads of her line of sight.

"I'm afraid of who I am," she whispered, wreathing her arms about herself as she netted their eyes together.

He was silent and would only listen, as he had a precarious feeling no one ever heard her.

"I don't know who I am," Roxanne said, a pious grieving on her tongue that made Finn understand that what she told him had never before left the cage inside her head.

A pale sliver of sunset cast a hollow of light like a halo on her face and Finn found she stole his breath.

"I can't remember," she murmured. "I can't remember who I am. It's like I didn't exist until two years ago when I suddenly woke up."

Finn narrowed his brow as her tongue fell still.

"What... what do you mean?" he stumbled. "You don't remember anything before two years ago?"

Roxanne slowly shook her head and he could see the fear in her eyes, even as she tried to hide them from him.

"All I know is that two years ago yesterday I woke up alone in this very flat," she said. "I had no name, no past, no memory. It was like someone was playing a trick on me. For the first year I kept waiting for them to jump out of the closet and say 'gotcha!'"

She brushed a fleet hand across her eyes and sat down on the bench of the windowsill, folding her hands in her lap and dropping her eyes to her bare toes. Even in the generous folds of Finn's jacket she was shivering, like she was naked in a snowstorm.

"The only name that made any kind of sense to me when I really tried to think of it was Roxanne," she said slowly, the tethers of her voice wandering. "I know downstairs it says 'R. LaMotte' and I know that logically I should deduce that that means that *I'm*

R. LaMotte, but that just doesn't feel like my name. R. LaMotte is a stranger."

Finn ran a hand across his beleaguered eyes and took a heavy seat beside her, leaving a noticeable distance between them. Roxanne leaned her elbows on her knees and laid her head into her palms, masking the wet lashes of her eyes behind fingers that faintly trembled.

"What I do know," she breathed. "I know no mail comes to me. Not bills or junk mail or anything. I don't even pay rent, like I've been forgotten. I know that before two years ago there must have been a man living here because I found a shaving kit under the bathroom sink. And I know that now I am alone."

Finn drew a sharp breath.

"You aren't alone," he said. The heaviness of her pain weighed his voice down like lead.

What kind of trauma would cause her to forget herself yet leave her in one piece? What kind of tragedy was it that she would rather live as a ghost than remember?

Roxanne glanced sideways at him, a bitterly wistful smile upon her mouth, tears like pearls in her eyes.

"I've stopped expecting that I'll remember someday," she said, her voice steeped in weariness. "I know I have to move on, start over, but it's like I'm stuck. I can't go back and I can't move forward, and the present that I'm in is nothingness. I think, if I had family, why haven't they found me yet? Or am I even being looked for? Why did they leave me? What did I do? Then I get scared and I don't want them to find me, or to find them myself, because I don't want to know why. I don't want to know why I've been alone."

Roxanne slowly pushed the jacket sleeves up to her elbows and raised her bound wrists up to her eyes.

"I didn't think anyone would notice that I was gone," she whispered. "I don't remember cutting so many times. Just this weakness, like falling asleep."

"You don't have to tell me this," Finn quickly said as he saw the bristled shivering in her long, thin fingers.

"I said I would," Roxanne told him, "when I realized why."

She silenced him with a sallow urgency in her voice and he gave her his attention.

"I'm not afraid anymore," she said. "Death is the last thing we face that we truly fear. But there's nothing to it that you have to be afraid of. I lived my death and I know it's not to fear. So now there is nothing holding me down, except myself."

Finn leaned forward pensively.

"But how do you start again when you can't remember where you began?" he asked. "There's a process to these things, people you can see who can help you."

Roxanne cut him off with a grievous shake of her head.

"I don't want that," she told him adamantly. "I don't want to be sealed in a tiny room with a shrink who thinks he knows better than I what suffering is, because he has a diploma hanging in a frame on the wall above his head; who thinks I'm crazy; who thinks he can fix me by pretending he understands. I'm not broken. I don't need to be fixed. Well, I *am* broken but I don't need an analysis."

Her voice ebbed off her tongue and she clamped her mouth shut, afraid of where she was going.

"You can't do this on your own, Roxanne," Finn said, unable to comprehend her chosen solitude even as he recognized it as his own.

"But I'm not," she murmured, her eyes on him brimming. "That's why I know I can do it. You're here. As far as I know, you're the first. As far as I know, you're the only person I've had contact with my entire life. When I called you, you were there. You found me, Finnean. I understand why. I didn't get it until last night. I was a ghost because I was alone, because I chose to have it so. Because I was still afraid."

Roxanne caught his stare on her, rapt as though she cast a spell upon him, and she shook her head, suddenly inhibited.

"Now I'm rambling," she sighed bitter sweetly, her trembling fingers on her brow. "There's so much in my head but it's like wet paint in my mouth. Everything is a choice. I chose solitude. I have chosen not to remember. I chose to slash my wrists. But I did choose to call you, too. And you chose to come. And it's fear that motivates it all."

Roxanne sighed heavy as stone, her breath shuddering beneath the weight of her torment so long shut in, like a sickness that finally breaks the barrier of one's health to consume them whole.

"But I couldn't have called you had I not slashed my wrists," she said with abrupt clarity, "had I not purged that fear... had I not chosen to do so."

She looked to Finn beside her, whose vast stare was frozen on nothingness in front of them. She could see the tempest that swelled beneath him.

"That is why I did it," Roxanne whispered. She leaned nearer to him, intrigued by the pensive trance in his eyes. "But because I felt you holding my hand, because you wouldn't let me leave, I'm still alive. When it is my time, the only things that will matter are what's in my heart, and what I choose to do with them."

Finn was silent. Something she had said triggered something in him he did not expect, something he believed he had long left behind. It was only buried deep within him and now it was reeling against the cage of his ribs like the last throes of a hooked fish. He had chosen his own wretched solitude and when she called him, he had chosen to answer her and face it again.

And now she had spilled herself on him. She was naked. He couldn't leave her like that.

"I haven't spoken to my brother in seven years," he said, his own voice startling him, trapped, as it had been, inside his head.

Roxanne didn't move and watched his mouth as he spoke, his eyes fixed on the floor, lost on the current of his own words.

"He's three years older," Finn continued, his jaw set with some deep-rooted affliction, tattooed like a map beneath his skin. "Our dad left when I was just young, before I could really remember him. Mum had to work two jobs and my brother practically raised me. He became a freelance journalist and I followed his footsteps. I was working with him for the first time when I found out he was using.

He laughed at me when I confronted him about it. He laughed at me...."

He sighed wearily, folding his hands together and leaning his chin on his thumbs, sure even Roxanne could feel the weight of his past, like chains, upon him.

"I watched it taking all of him," he whispered. "I watched it destroy him until it was all that mattered to him. For a year I watched it eat him whole. We were in Berlin when we heard our mother had died. I thought that would change things and I was right. He left. One day he was just... gone, every trace of him. What he didn't take, I... I used. I didn't know then what it meant."

The shame in his voice was toxic and Roxanne had to look away.

"I didn't see him again for a year," Finn said. "When I did, he had entered a rehab program and was clean. I couldn't go a day without it. I used to keep it in old Tylenol and pill bottles in my medicine cabinet. He had his life back and I was an addict. That was the last time we spoke. I lost my job, any friends I had ever made. I lost my soul. That's what happens. You forget you're even human, even alive. All you care about is the next hit and how you're going to get it. I pawned the diamond from our mother's wedding ring for a fifty. It was worth ten times that but I didn't care, not at the time. Now I can't believe I did that. He's married with three kids now, my brother. I've never seen my nieces."

Finn brushed a hand across his weathered eyes and leaned back against the window, pulling his shirtsleeves up above his elbows so she could see the tiny, pin prick-like scars that peppered his arms.

"It almost killed me at least half a dozen times," he breathed, the mettle drained from his voice. "The last time I was in the hospital it was because I'd had a minor heart attack. I was told that if I continued using, I could be dead within weeks, days even. I didn't care about life but I didn't want to die, so a few years ago I locked myself in the bathroom and didn't come out again until I stopped shaking. I almost killed myself, but I've not touched it since. I still want it every day, though. Every day."

"You beat it," Roxanne whispered.

"I won the battle but the war's not over," he told her with a listless grin that held no amusement. "I'm scared one day I won't be strong enough. Because it's always there. It's my shadow. I won't ever get away from it."

"And you're punishing yourself for that?" she asked softly.

Finn glanced at her sharply.

"You live your own isolation," she said. "Just like me."

He felt a faint smile warm his face.

"And I thought we were oil and water."

Roxanne mirrored his weary grin and slid her back against the window.

"So, what happens when two lost souls meet?" she asked, leaning her head on the chill of the glass.

"I don't know," Finn sighed. "I've never known one long enough to know for sure."

Roxanne smiled, her eyes on the floor demurely lit, and he could feel the hesitance on her tongue before she slowly moved her hand over his and laid her fingers across his knuckles. Her palm was cold as ice on his skin and he wreathed her hand in both of his. He netted her in his eyes, his fingertips gently stroking the soft bandages around her wrists, but she wouldn't look at him. A pale scarlet blushed across her ashy cheeks and in the cradle of his fingers he could feel her hand shivering.

"You do know you've completely captivated me," Finn told her suddenly, startling himself even as his voice tumbled out of his mouth.

But she smiled, shy and happily, her teeth like pearls, and even with her gaze turned down from him, he could see that it danced.

She nodded faintly and held her breath, waver in the frozen tightness across her shoulders. Inside her head, she was still deciding.

But Finn's eyes on her felt warm, a gentleness she had forgotten, and there was nothing else then. As though the whole of the world had stopped spinning, the frail traffic on the street below halted and sirens in the distance waned with the strangle of faraway voices. When the earth began to turn again it was only for two lonely heartbeats. All else had left them and all she could feel was him beside her.

Roxanne looked up into the vastness of his stare and knew how deep the well of his torture went, knew it because it matched the doom of her own, though she had no memory of it. The bible of his torment gave her own its voice.

Roxanne locked his eyes to hers and glided against him, her hands heavy on his shoulders. She sank into his lap and felt her breath burdening, her ribs reeling as he watched her with a kindled surprise that softly waned. Neither looked away as he peeled the jacket from her shoulders and pushed it down her arms, the tickle of his fingertips on her skin wringing at the corners of her mouth. As the coat pooled on the floor over his feet he pressed his palms on the small of her back and hesitantly drew her nearer, half expecting her to back out of his hands. But instead he felt her fingers on his throat, mapping his jaw.

Neither shut their eyes as she leaned against him and laid her mouth on his, his lips frail as a whisper. Her face bleared in his gaze and all he could feel was her mouth, cold and parched on his, all he could hear, his heart pounding against the rungs of his ribcage like urgent fists on a door shut and barred.

When she pulled back, he could still feel her breath in his mouth and his head was stumbling to catch her. In the corset of his arms, she was weightless.

When she bent to kiss him again, her eyes were closed.

Chapter Eight

She stared at the ceiling. Finn lay beside her, his head on her shoulder, his finger tracing the outline of her hand laid flat across her belly. The bristle of his hair tickled her chin and she could feel his smell of soap and sweat on her skin. He was warm against her, his breath stroking her chest, and she shuttered her eyes and sighed.

Finn drew his fingers across a long, narrow scar cut into Roxanne's abdomen and pondered out loud.

"What's this from?" he asked, his voice threading the stillness.

Roxanne shook her head. She had wondered after it herself.

"I don't know," she murmured.

"It looks like a medical scar."

"Haven't you any scars you can't remember?"

Finn lifted his head and leaned his chin on the ledge of her shoulder, her face filling his eyes as he threaded their hands together across her stomach.

"No," he said. "They're not many. I remember them."

Roxanne smiled and opened her eyes, tilting her head down at him.

"Were you a sheltered child?" she asked, her voice faintly teasing.

She brushed her fingers across a small scar above his eyebrow. "What is this one from?"

"Bar fight," Finn told her, his brow furrowed in feigned earnestness.

She laughed, laying her palm against the side of his face and holding it there. Finn smiled and sighed with rough defeat.

"I was running from a dog," he relented. "I tried climbing over a fence and landed face first into a gardening spade."

Roxanne narrowed her eyes in amused sympathy.

"You could have lost your eye," she said, her voice soothing as though he still felt the pain of it.

"I nearly did," he mumbled. "And it was my dog, too."

He rose on an elbow and leaned his head against his hand to look down on her.

"Could you love me if I only had one eye?" he asked.

"If you only had one of everything," she said, "I could still love you."

Finn bent and kissed her.

"Could you love me if I knew who I was?" Roxanne asked as he drew back.

He smiled and nodded as he traced the curve of her bottom lip with his thumb.

"Yes," he said. "I will."

"Even if I'm married or something?"

"I'd fight your husband for you."

Her face shadowed and she averted her eyes.

"I'm afraid to find out," she admitted.

"Do you truly want to?" Finn asked.

"Don't you want me to?"

"If you do."

Roxanne reached up and brushed her mouth across his, tracing the parched outline of her lips on his.

"If you help me," she said. "I can't do this on my own."

"You won't," he told her without waver.

Finn smiled.

"That wasn't so difficult, was it?" he said. "Asking for help. It is free, you know."

"Nothing's free," Roxanne murmured.

He cradled his arm over her chest and she kissed the inside of his elbow, lightly pressing her mouth over the scars that blackened his skin like tiny bruises.

"I could be a serial killer on the lam," she whispered, "on the run from the law."

"Cool," Finn said. "I've always wanted to know someone famous."

She laughed softly and brushed her palm back and forth across his forearm until he felt his skin grow hot beneath the pulse of her hand.

"Did you know all along this would happen?" she asked. "This: you and I..."

"No," he told her. "This was a surprise."

"Did you want it?"

"Yes."

"I love how you're honest with me."

"I've no reason to lie," he said. "That comes later, *after* I get to know you."

Roxanne laughed again and he felt her last walls against him crumbling to the strings of her own voice.

Her expression went slack and she looked sad and lonely again.

"I wish you could be as honest with yourself," she said.

Finn furrowed his brow.

"What do you mean?"

"I mean your brother," she told him. "I mean, if I could really remember my family I think I'd do anything to connect with them again, no matter what they'd done to me or I to them."

She felt him instantly bristle.

"Well, you don't remember, do you," he said, his voice bristling as he recoiled his arms from about her and lay flat at her side.

"Wow," she breathed. "That will leave a scar I'll remember."

Finn sighed and laid a hand across his eyes.

"I didn't mean—"

"No," she cut him off. "You knew it would hurt me and it did. And you said it anyway."

"A few hours ago you said you didn't want to know your family," he told her.

Roxanne's eyes flared wide.

"Something of some significance to me has happened since then," she hissed. "I've realized just how big a hole being alone has buried in me. I thought you understood that."

"You know I do," he said. "I just don't need you telling me about a wound of which you have no idea how deep really goes."

Roxanne turned onto her side and stared down at him, her eyes cold.

"I felt it when you spoke of him," she said. "I could hear the regret in your voice."

Finn sat up sharply, catching her off guard.

"You're lecturing me about regret," he said bluntly, feeling ill by the abrasive cruelty he heard spout off his own tongue that he couldn't stop. "You who haven't a past."

Roxanne sat up beside him.

"This is what you do, isn't it," she said. "Your hackles go up when you hear something you don't want to and you revert to pathetic victim pouring salt on wounds you already know are there. You really don't fight fair."

"You want to talk about pathetic?" Finn asked, locking her stare to his. "Who's wearing bloody tourniquets but can't even spell out a good enough reason to want to die? The fight isn't fair because you're wrong. You want to immerse yourself into my life so you won't have to face your own. You're scared to find out who you are, even though I told you I'd be with you, too scared to see if you even have a family you left behind so you'll take mine. You know, you would have been enough for me."

"It isn't nice going to bed with Mysterious Stranger and waking up next to me, is it," Roxanne said bitterly, fighting hot tears in her eyes as her throat burned.

"That's not what this is about," he told her.

"Isn't it. But now that you've gotten what you wanted and you're hearing what you don't want to hear, you're suddenly wearing so much armor I can't even see you."

"*You're* hearing what you don't want to. And now the defenses are back up and no matter what I say it'll be an attack. I'm assuming this comes tragically natural to you or do you mean to be so guarded."

"Have I no reasons to be guarded? I'm not completely sure that's a flaw."

"Trust me, it is."

"I *did* trust you."

Finn was about to spit fire back at her when the hollow tenor of her voice hit his head like kids throwing stones at a window, and he heard her torture like a sickness in her throat.

This frail web of her life was all she had. Every wall and every reason was just.

"But, like everything else apparently, I was wrong," Roxanne murmured, the fight ebbed from her voice, enduring only sadness. "Serves me right, I guess. The first person I give all of me to throws it all back."

"I'm not throwing anything back," Finn told her slowly. "You're taking it from me."

"Maybe I wouldn't, if you'd fight harder."

"It seems it's the fight that's taking you away."

"There are different kinds of fighting."

"But you won't let me. You won't let me fight for you because you've already convinced yourself you aren't worthy. You can't let yourself be at peace. You've lived this nightmare so long, it's a comfort to you now. It's your security. Someone else can't hurt you if you're all alone. Fear motivates everything and it's all you have inside you."

Roxanne choked.

"Fear? Fear keeps you from the family you know."

"It wasn't fear that led me to you."

"Then we are wrong. Fear doesn't control us. Unless it *was* fear that drove you to me. Unless you're just a liar."

"Look, the whole fear-motivates-our-every-move speech is bullshit. I *wanted* you, Roxanne. You're the most beautiful thing I've ever seen, even as sad and twisted with grief as you are. And when you became real to me, I fell in love with you."

Anguished tears flooded her eyes, like the direness in his voice was shredding her. She looked made of broken glass fit back together, that even the frailest touch or breath would shatter again.

"Well, that was your mistake, wasn't it," she told him. Her voice barely squeezed through the constricted tunnel of her throat as she fought the swells of emotion that were causing her entire body to shiver.

Heartbreak scored Finn's face and made his eyes burn.

"Why are you doing this?"

Roxanne tucked her legs up against her chest and laid her cheek on her knees, refusing to look at him even as she felt his eyes goring into the side of her face.

"Do you want me to leave?"

She suddenly stabbed him with her bleary eyes.

"Yes," she told him acidly, her tongue plunging like a blunt knife. "This was *my* mistake."

Finn hadn't expected that and he felt the sting of her embittered rejection like poison.

"I don't think I should leave you alone," he said.

Roxanne stroked hot tears from her cheeks with trembling fingers.

"Why?" she asked, her voice wet and shivering. "Because I might try to kill myself?"

"It wouldn't be the first time."

He couldn't misread the injury in her eyes.

"I'm sorry, Roxanne," he said, his voice instantly softened.

"But that's the problem," she told him, her face turned away. "I'm not."

Finn watched her for a moment but she was cold. She was shut.

He slowly gathered up his clothes and didn't look back at her as he made his way to the door. He knew she wouldn't be looking after him.

He stopped in the kitchen, the knife in the sink snagging his eyes. He knew she wouldn't, but he snatched the knife up into his hand anyway on his way out the door.

Chapter Nine

Finn slammed the door to his apartment so hard that it made the walls shudder. His whole body trembled with anger. He tossed Roxanne's knife onto the counter and grabbed the toaster, tearing the plug from the socket as he threw the appliance across the kitchen. It slammed into the wall with a tinny thud as the mechanisms inside snapped loose and came apart.

Mad hot adrenalin was coursing through his veins. Tossing the toaster had only briefly dispelled it. He clutched the edge of the counter like he meant to tear it apart. He clutched his chest and inhaled deeply. His heart was racing. He was out of breath, with the weak muscle working double time to tame both the agony and the anger of rejection that was boiling him from the inside out.

His chest cavity ached. He had to calm down. But all he wanted to do was rage. All he wanted to do was tear himself apart, or someone else.

He hadn't let Roxanne see his anger, or the torturous hurt she caused. No woman had exposed these weaknesses of character in him before. No woman was capable. No woman was Roxanne. She was still holding his still-beating heart in her hand.

He told her he loved her. The words had just tumbled out of

his mouth before the little synapses in his brain could even recognize them. He had meant it. He did love her. He truly did. He had said those words before but they had never been more than just a sequence of sounds. They had never before been more than just a tool. But he was on fire for Roxanne and every sinew, fiber and inch of himself had meant those words. Which made the sting of her rejection all the more destructive.

Finn looked up. Dovey Charles's white china plate was sitting on the counter, staring back at him like an empty eye socket. He straightened and rubbed the blear from his eyes on the sleeve of his shirt. Roxanne's knife and Dovey's plate. He glanced up at the ceiling but not a creak of the floorboards or a dash of Roxanne's footsteps had he heard since leaving her apartment. It was like she wasn't even up there, or, worse, that she knew he would be listening for her and was being silent just because she knew it would torment him.

Finn grabbed Dovey's plate. He crossed the hall and knocked resolutely on her door, his expression fixed with determination. She answered after just a moment, her eyes sparkling with saccharine surprise.

"Finn," she said. His name in her mouth sounded like she was running silk over her tongue.

"Hi, Dovey," he said. "I know it's late, but I thought I'd bring back your plate."

Dovey's smile was dazzling, but it had always been dazzling. Warmth bloomed across her face and she stood aside.

"Well, then you better come in," she said.

Finn stepped around her and she shut the door behind him. He had never been inside her apartment before, and not for her lack of inviting him. It was so neat and orderly. He didn't know how she had done it, but it had a perfect balance of comfort and esthetic, with furniture that was both architecturally beautiful and inviting. It looked like a show room of her life and he wondered where the clutter was, proverbial and otherwise. Did she actually live like this, or had she known he would come?

This apartment was welcoming and warm, just like Dovey herself. This was the apartment of someone who was settled, who had peace. It made him think of Roxanne, whose place was cold and bereft of mementos, and of his own, which mirrored the sparseness of his nomadic soul. It further cemented his feeling that he and Roxanne were alone in the world but for each other.

Finn turned around and found Dovey standing in his shadow, so near she almost startled him.

"I'm glad you decided to come by," she said.

Her nearness made him uncomfortable, like the air was too close for him to breathe properly. The fact that he was shut with her alone in her apartment made the situation seem a lot more intimate than what he had been prepared for. He swallowed hard and brought the plate up in between them. Without taking her eyes from him, she took the plate from his hands and set it down on the counter beside them.

"Zachary's at my mother's," she said, "all weekend."

Finn smiled unsurely as she took a step nearer to him. She was so close her body was a breath away from brushing up against his.

"He's a good kid," he said.

"I do my best," she told him. "It's a source of personal pride with me that I do the best in every aspect of my life."

She laid her hand on his arm. He glanced down at it.

"*Every* aspect?" he asked.

She smiled and nodded her head. Her hand travelled up his bicep, over his shoulder, and settled at the back of his neck. Her fingers softly strummed the notch of his spine and sent a shiver racing down his back.

"Why don't you let me show you," she purred.

Dovey pressed her body against him, pulled his head down towards her, and locked her mouth over his. Surprise caught him off balance and he had to grab onto her to keep from staggering backwards. Her lips were soft and pliable and her tongue twisted around his like a pretzel. Her body heat soaked through her clothing and burned his palms. When she pulled away, he was stunned for several seconds and slowly shook the daze from his head.

"What, just like that?" he asked. "You don't want to talk or anything?"

Dovey coiled her arms around his neck and stood up on the tips of her toes.

"I'm a thirty-one-year-old, single mother still paying off my student loans," she told him. "I don't have the luxury of being coy or patient. Right now I just want you to kiss me, Finn."

He stared at her for a moment. She couldn't have made it easier for him. Dovey was beautiful, kind and willing; more than willing, she wanted him.

Finn folded her in his arms and laid his mouth over hers. She responded eagerly and he could feel energy coursing between them.

"Take me to the sofa," she whispered in his ear, her breath hot and damp on his skin.

Finn lifted her off the floor and carried her to the sofa. He laid her on the cushions and she pulled him down on top of her, wrapping her legs around his waist to pin him there.

Finn's head was in a fog. He couldn't think straight. He didn't even know what he was doing. Dovey was like clay in his hands. He could mould and shape her to his liking. She could be anyone for him. She would do anything for him. But he didn't want Dovey. He didn't love Dovey, and his anger over Roxanne had already evaporated.

Roxanne. His heart did a cartwheel at the thought of her. Dovey Charles was in his mouth but couldn't tremble him like the very thought of Roxanne.

What was he doing? Less than an hour before he had been with someone he loved and now he was spitting on what that had meant to him. Kissing Dovey was not like kissing Roxanne. Kissing Dovey was not hurting Roxanne; it was hurting himself and the fact that he only wanted to kiss Roxanne and Roxanne alone for the rest of his life. He wasn't going to make that happen being angry or taking his frustrations out on Dovey. Both women deserved better from him.

When Dovey's hands slid over his stomach to the clasp of his belt, Finn broke free.

"Wait," he said, fishing her hands out from underneath him. "Dovey, wait. Are you sure?"

Confusion dampened Dovey's heat mottled features, then realization made her face fall. He wasn't asking her if she was sure; he was telling her that he wasn't.

"Yes," she told him, "but you're not."

As tears dotted her blue irises, she pulled herself out from underneath him and they sat side by side on the edge of the sofa. He hung his brow into his hands and shook his head.

"I'm sorry, Dovey," he murmured. "We can't do this; *I* can't do this."

Dovey's bottom lip began to tremble and she buttoned up her blouse with a blush of humiliation burning across the bridge of her nose.

"It was completely unfair of me to come over tonight," he told her. Anxiety made his voice tremble. "This wasn't about you. Look, you're great, Dovey. You're sweet and beautiful and generous. It's just..."

A look that was half a bitter smile and half a sweet grimace hooded Dovey's expression. She reached out and laid her hand over his, which was jittering on top of his knee.

"But I'm not who you want," she said.

Pain shot across his face as he met her blue stare.

"I'm sorry," he said again.

His voice was drenched with earnestness. It made her eyes water but she squeezed his hand and braced herself and kept the tears from falling.

"I wish things could be different," she said.

He smiled sadly at her.

"So do I sometimes. Being with you, Dovey, it would be easy but it's not what I want. I could never be who you need me to be. I don't want you to waste your time waiting for me. You might miss out on someone else, someone right."

Dovey only nodded and turned her eyes away. He watched a single tear slide down the profile of her cheekbone.

"Why do you like me anyway?" he asked.

She smiled and wiped the tear away.

"Are you kidding?" she said. "Have you looked at yourself in the mirror lately? You're like a less feminine Johnny Depp. All the women in the building would have given their right breast to be me five minutes ago." She turned and faced him. Warmth had seeped back into her features. "You're good to my son," she told him. "And he likes you. I melt for any man who can make my son smile."

"Can I ask you a personal question?" Finn said.

Dovey regarded him cautiously for a moment before nodding her head.

"Where's Zachary's father?" he asked.

Sadness peppered her eyes. She looked down at her left hand and twisted an invisible ring around her finger.

"He left us," she said. "It was an aneurism, in his brain. He just dropped dead one day. Zach was around two."

Sympathy scored Finn's eyes.

"I'm sorry, Dovey," he murmured.

He laid a comforting hand on her shoulder and she looked up at him, her blue eyes glittering.

"You remind me of him," she said. "He was the love of my life and I lost him. I already lost him."

Pain slivered Finn's tongue.

"I'm sorry," he whispered.

"That's all you can say, isn't it?" she murmured.

They looked at each other.

"You hide your pain so well, Dovey," he told her.

"Of course I do," she said. "I was trying to attract you. What man wants an emotional mess, least of all an emotional mess with a child? You don't, by the way, hide your pain so well. That's why you want to be alone, isn't it?"

Finn's eyes wandered.

"Is it?" He seemed to be asking himself.

Dovey searched his face.

"What happened to you, Finn?" she asked. "You aren't the same man you were last week."

He smiled sadly.

"Is that a good or bad thing?" he asked.

She was quiet and he glanced back at her. She seemed to be trying to decide. Then she smiled at him.

"I think it's a good thing." Her smile bittered a little but she didn't brush it away. "It's her, isn't it? The woman you went to the hospital with?"

He slowly nodded his head and Dovey's expression turned tender.

"I think you love her," she said. "I think that's what's different about you."

"It's complicated," he told her uneasily.

"Isn't it always? I wish I could have been the one for you."

"Don't be. I probably saved you a lot of grief."

"Is that how you really feel about it? Is that why you're really here with me?"

Shame clouded Finn's expression.

"I wanted to hurt her," he said.

"Finn, if there's one thing I know for sure it's that if you can feel pain, you can feel happiness, too," she told him.

"I did feel happiness."

"And she was the reason?"

"Yes."

"So what are you still doing here?"

"I told you. It's—"

"Complicated," she interrupted him. "Yeah, I got that. So go. Stop bending my ear and go uncomplicate it."

"I don't know how," he told her with frustration.

"Then you're going to lose her."

He glanced at her sharply.

"I know," he said.

Finn rose to his feet. Dovey's eyes followed him and he looked down at her.

"I'm sorry you lost your husband," he said. "But you're a good person, Dovey. You shouldn't hide yourself."

She smiled up at him.

"You know? You could have strung me along for a *little* while longer," she said. "Aren't you tempted?"

He looked at her for a moment. There was still an ember of sad hope in her diamond blue eyes. He shook his head and snuffed it.

"Not to hurt you," he told her. He leaned down and kissed her softly on the cheek. "Good-bye, Dovey," he whispered.

Dovey watched him turn away and walk to the front door. His hand on the brass knob, he glanced back at her and she smiled for him. Then he shut the door.

❧

A day passed, then another. Finn sat in front of the blank screen of his computer and tried not to listen for her. He filled his head with her instead. He still wanted her, wanted her with him. He still wanted to know who she was.

But he couldn't go to Roxanne like this. Not after the things he had said to her. Not after Dovey. Not empty handed.

It was stabbing at his head. The scar across her belly, stitched fine and precise. Too precise for an accident of some kind. It had to be a medical scar, and if it was, there would be a record of it somewhere.

It cuffed him like a slap across his face: a cesarean scar. Roxanne had a child!

Chapter Ten

She waited out the day, wrapped inside her bedclothes like a butterfly in its cocoon. Once, she took her tent out into the kitchen and stood in front of the stuck drawer. She wrapped her fingers around the knob and took a deep breath as she pulled on it. The drawer didn't budge an inch and she retreated back to her bed.

She wondered if this was what it was like not to be alone. She wondered if men and women were tragically fated to burn each other up, like God—was there such divinity?—was only playing a joke to see how long it would take until they got it. She didn't think it was funny, although when she stepped outside of herself and examined the human race like from the birds' point of view to the ants, she could see the sick humor of it. She decided life was like a Shakespearean comedy. You are told that it's working comic genius and you nod in agreement even though you silently don't really get it.

They were all so flawed. She wondered if they could ever heal and she wondered if it was even worth bothering to try. It was all so cruel, to agonize so much for so little gain and reward. What was gained and what rewards were given could just so easily be snatched away again, most likely by the one who did the giving in the first place. Or so it seemed to Roxanne.

So much grief for what she didn't know. Perhaps it was better this way, to never know what she had lost. Perhaps it was best to be alone. One cannot mourn what one never had to begin with.

She didn't know why Finn's face filled her mind then. She didn't understand why he was in her head, why when she thought of him, it pulled at the corners of her mouth. But, maybe she did. Maybe she knew and was afraid. She had felt the kindness in his heart, the kind one cannot hide or disguise, long before she heard his name. And now in his leaving she mourned him. Was this what it was to love, feeling hot and cold at the same time? Roxanne could only guess.

But she wanted to learn all of him, all of who he was and who he used to be. She wanted to memorize the lament of his youth and envision the man he would become five years from this moment. Every wound ever inflicted made him so. Had she loved him always? She had first seen him checking his mail and watched as he did, as he juggled the parchments in between his fingers; the face he made when he came across one letter in particular; the way his forehead knotted and his eyes crinkled.

He had been so careful with her, like he feared she would break apart in his hands. She felt she knew herself when she was with him. When he had been lying beside her, her skin warmed with his nearness, she hadn't been afraid.

The only other time she had been so completely without fear was when she had felt all the life ebbing away from her; when she could no longer feel the grooves of the floorboards against her bones or the heavy, hot wetness crawling on her flesh or the pain, dull as an echo, writhing just beneath her skin; when she had been faraway and she didn't feel her body, only the anchor of her heartbeat.

There was nothingness for a long time, as though she floated on her back on the ocean, her eyes shut up at a sky charred with storm clouds. Then there was a voice from somewhere beyond herself and a pressure on her hand pulling her back down inside the shell of her body; someone's hand knotted around hers. Then she was afraid, afraid to die and never know whose hand it was. Roxanne believed it had been at that moment that she had decided she would live.

Chapter Eleven

Finn paced the hospital corridor like a newborn father, a hand at his mouth, teeth gnawing at a fingernail. He could feel the lump of his heart in his throat and his ribs ached.

This was all he had. This was all he could do for her. If this hunch didn't pan out, he had nothing left to offer her to let him stay. He never got hunches, so he couldn't trust himself with this one, but he wanted, unlike anything else, to believe. It was for her, for this frail hope he couldn't keep from stirring in the back of his head, like a tattered rag churning in the current of the wind.

Finn lamented the words he said to her but strangely found he couldn't repent them. She was most alive when she was persecuted, when she felt she had to fight or defend herself. He wondered why that was. What great ill had she suffered? Whose betrayal was it that poisoned her trust? She *had* been betrayed. Finn could see the scar tissue of that wound in her eyes when they would well and she would look almost puzzled as though she didn't know why. There was a great and deep trauma, somewhere inside her, on her soul, bleeding into her veins like a sickness.

A door opened down the hall and Finn met the lab-coat clad man, tall and four eyed, half way, embittered anxiety stirring his haste. The man carried a folder in the crook of one arm.

Finn's nerve was on fire.

"You found it?" he spurred breathlessly.

The man was still, his eyes on Finn, watching him closely, and for a moment Finn couldn't breathe. Then the man sighed and held out the folder in both of his hands, Finn's wide eyes upon it livid with anxiety.

"I'm just a chemist," the man said. "I could get fired for this."

Finn barely heard him.

"There's a much better place waiting for you, Lewis," he said.

"I don't think, actually, that stealing confidential personal files from the place of my employment qualifies me for a front row seat in the Great Beyond," Lewis said. "They already don't like me here and now I've gone and committed a felony. This makes us even... Are you listening to me?"

"What?"

Finn's eyes slowly panned up into Lewis's menacing glare.

"This makes us even, Finn," he said slowly, his tongue deliberate.

"Of course, of course," Finn told him laboriously. "You never gave me this and I don't know you."

"What do you want with it, anyway?"

"It isn't for me."

"That makes me feel better."

Lewis hesitated, his fingers bound about the folder like the pins of a lock.

"It's for her?" he asked, his fingertips tapping the skin of the file.

"What's with the questions, Lewis?" Finn said, his timbre darkening.

"I promised your brother I'd ask after you if I ever saw you again," Lewis told him.

Finn swore beneath his breath and laid a hand across his wearied eyes.

"Well, you *didn't* see me."

"If I did, I might have to tell him why, and I'd prefer this stay between the two of us."

Finn sighed and felt his tattered breath grate against his ribcage.

"You should call him," Lewis said.

"You got him clean," Finn told him. "You've done enough for him."

"You can't do *everything* yourself, Finnean," Lewis said.

Finn was still for a moment.

"No," he said quietly. "I know that."

Lewis furrowed his brow at the hazy depth of Finn's stare and struggled to see not the junkie but the man. It was the first time he was able to do it, to believe he was no longer lost, as Lewis had only known him, to believe he was no longer a ghost.

Lewis slowly let his fingers unclench and held the file out for Finn to take, near startling him as he did.

"I am sorry, Finn."

"For what?"

Lewis shook his head.

"I never believed you would do it," he said, "on your own like you did."

Finn was unapologetic.

"I know," he said. "But don't beat yourself up. It was full, the house of people who never did. That's probably why I'm still alive. Had to prove you were all wrong." He looked up into Lewis' eyes. "Hey, is your brother still working Vice?"

Lewis' expression turned suspicious.

"Yeah," he said slowly. "Why?"

"He might like to know there's a dealer selling to pre-teens out in Fisher Park," Finn told him. "Maybe you could let him know for me."

Lewis slowly nodded, his eyes still frosted over with apprehension.

"Okay, thanks," Finn said.

He slowly took the folder into his hands, careful, as though it was fragile, as though it would tear apart in his fingers, and walked away. He was going to discover all of her in these pages, all of which she didn't know and all of what she didn't have.

He suddenly wanted to rip it up, only to prove to her that it didn't matter. Written words on a page didn't make her who she was. What could words tell him that he didn't already know? Too long had he loved her as a shadow, too long had she been one.

Finn sat on the park bench, his hands in his pockets. His leg shook restlessly up and down. He stared out at the small, rock-walled pond. A skin of ice had formed on its surface. Several ducks, fat with down, were paddling around a clear spot in the middle.

The folder sat beside him on the bench. He didn't look at it; he hadn't opened it yet; he didn't know if he could. He didn't even know if he could face her again; their last encounter ended so abruptly and so badly. And what happened with Dovey made him feel guilty. Would he even be able to look Roxanne in the eye?

He was afraid; of that Finn was certain. He was afraid of what might happen if the truth took Roxanne away; afraid of what *he* might do; afraid his strength of will might finally abandon him; afraid his hounding demon might defeat him at last. What if this past that she had forgotten had no place for him? What if he would lose her to her memories? Could he risk that? He could make her his forever. He could return to her and make it better and they could be together, together in ignorance.

But even as Finn thought that, he knew it wasn't possible.

He was half tempted to toss the folder in the trash bin beside the bench. He was half tempted to walk back home, back to Roxanne, and never speak of it again. He was half tempted.

Finn looked down at the folder. He slowly extracted his hands from the pockets of his coat and picked it up. It was surprisingly heavy and he grimaced with distress; that couldn't be a good thing.

He opened the file and began to read. Minutes later, he began to cry.

Chapter Twelve

Finn parked his car on the curb and checked and rechecked the address. The brick townhouse was on a quiet, oak-lined street, the skeletal branches of which were reaching over the street to clutch at their neighbors, forming a kind of arbor. A group of new mothers with strollers and big, purebred dogs were walking down the sidewalk. Finn let them pass before crossing the walkway and climbing the short flight of stairs. He rang the bell, heard it chime within, and exhaled a heavy, nervous breath.

After a minute, he heard locks clicking on the other side and the door opened. A young child stood in the threshold, looking up at him with a shy, curious smile and big, golden eyes.

For a moment, Finn's voice abandoned him. He was staring at a four-year-old version of Roxanne.

"You have your mother's eyes," he said.

Surprise dotted the girl's face and she eyed him suspiciously for just a second before her expression broke into a hyper wide grin.

"Nicola!"

The girl turned at the sound of the voice and an older woman with graying, buttercup-blonde hair appeared behind her. The woman held out her hand and the child took it. Her eyes on Finn were wary.

"Who are you?" she asked.

Finn inclined his head towards the little girl, still smiling up at him bright and sprightly.

"I know her mother," he said.

The color in the woman's expression paled and she looked with a start down at Nicola and back up to Finn.

"Nicola, go play in your room," she said.

Nicola looked up at her and tugged on the hem of the woman's shirt.

"But he says he knows Mummy," she told her.

"Now, Nicola."

Her voice was firm, inflexible, and Nicola hung her head with a pout, but obeyed. She pulled her little hand free, walked to the polished banister, and trudged up the stairs. Finn and the woman watched her until she disappeared, then slowly turned their eyes back to one another.

"Are you Helen?" he asked.

"Yes," she said. "Would you like to come in." It was a request rather than a question.

She stepped aside to allow Finn to walk past her, then shut the door.

"Bruce!" she called. She turned to Finn. "Can I take your coat?"

Finn shook his head.

"I can't stay long," he told her.

A man appeared, older, whose dark chestnut hair was flecked with white at the temples. He glanced between Finn and Helen unsurely, sharing the same stain of worry Helen herself wore.

"Who's this?" he asked.

Helen leaned close to him and murmured into his ear.

Bruce's attention snapped to Finn with a start. His eyes became sharp, almost predatory, and Finn almost took a step back.

"We haven't heard from her in two years," he said. "What do you want?"

His tone was defensive, confrontational. It made Finn prickle and the coldness Helen was forcing into her expression soured with distress.

"Bruce," she whispered gently, wringing her hands with concern.

Finn glanced back and forth between them and the heat on his face slowly cooled. Bewilderment took its place, then realization leached the color from his skin.

"You have no idea," he said. "You don't know what's been going on."

As Helen and Bruce exchanged a daunted look, Finn's gaze wandered. To the left of the foyer was a small, elegant sitting room. On top of the white marble fireplace sat a black and white photograph in a jet lacquer frame. His brow furrowed and he walked towards it. The alarm on Helen and Bruce's pallid faces intensified and they followed him.

Amazement spackled Finn's expression as he picked up the photograph and held it with both of his hands. He almost didn't recognize her. Roxanne's beaming face was staring out at him. Her hair was long and windswept, her smile so wide it engulfed her whole face. Even colorless, her eyes were sparkling; they were alive and dancing. She looked so happy, so soft; there was nothing hard or sharp or sad about her.

In her arms she carried a baby, no more than several weeks old, whose eyes were Roxanne's. Both of them were being cradled in the arms of a handsome, young man with effortlessly coifed hair, a square jaw and kind, light eyes. He was gazing at Roxanne as if the camera wasn't there at all. His expression was so unguarded, so true, it made Finn avert his eyes, as if this was a very intimate moment caught in time.

Anguish flogged his expression and he shut his eyes as he gently placed the picture back on the mantle. He slowly turned back around and found Helen and Bruce standing in the doorway. The lack of any comprehension on either of their faces made Finn's eyes water. He tried to rub the blear out on his fingers as he sat down on the edge of a baroque, hard-backed love seat, his knees shaking.

Bruce slowly came into the room and sat in one of the chairs opposite Finn. Finn was staring straight ahead into a haze of nothingness and Brice tried to intercept his line of sight and snag his attention.

"Who are you, son?" he asked. His voice had softened. Patience had seeped into it. "What's your name?"

Finn blinked and his eyes came into focus.

"Finn," he said.

Bruce looked up at the photograph that had snared Finn's eye, then back at Finn.

"Who are you to her?" he asked.

"I'm not sure," Finn murmured.

"Well, like I said, we're not in contact with her."

"Haven't you wondered why?" Sharpness severed all the civility out of Finn's voice. His suddenly livid eyes flashed back and forth between Helen and Bruce. "Haven't you wondered why you haven't heard from her in two years?"

Helen stepped into the room.

"I don't think we should be discussing this with you," she said, her voice trembling just a little. "We don't know you. And why isn't she here with you?"

"She doesn't know I'm here," Finn told her. "I wanted to know you before I went to her. I had to know."

"I don't understand," Helen said.

Finn set his jaw hard and stared at the polished hardwood floorboards between his feet.

"She doesn't know who you are." He began slowly, and had to fight to keep his voice steady and sure-footed. "She doesn't know that she's a mother. Two years ago she had an emotional breakdown. She doesn't remember anything before that."

Helen and Bruce's eyes snapped to one another as horrible disbelief washed over their faces and they shared a privately meaningful look.

"That's why you haven't heard from her in two years," Finn told them. "She doesn't know you exist."

Helen slowly sat rigidly into a chair beside her husband.

"You mean, she doesn't remember anything?" she asked. Her voice became more unhinged with anxiety with each word that passed her lips. "Not anything?"

Finn shook his head and tears bubbled into her eyes. Bruce was quiet. He leaned his chin into a hand and looked contemplative.

"Not Robert?" Helen asked. She pressed a hand across her mouth and breathed through the slats of her fingers. "Not Nicola?"

Finn shook his head again.

Bruce suddenly raised his eyes.

"What are you going to do now?" he asked.

There was fear in his voice. He tried to mask it by adopting an abrasive, accusatory tone, but Finn read through it; he recognized it.

"What do you mean?" he asked.

Bruce rose to his feet.

"Are you going to try to take her away?"

"Who?"

"Nicola!"

He barked the name and both Finn and Helen jumped with a start. She looked up at him, laid a soft hand on his arm, and tugged on his sleeve.

"Bruce, please..."

She tried to get him to sit back down but he pulled his arm free, his stare like a knife stabbing Finn between the eyes.

Finn felt his hackles go up.

"I'm not going to try to do anything," he said. "She's not my daughter. But she doesn't belong to you either."

"We've raised her since she was six months old," Bruce told him.

"Under the circumstances, you don't have the right to keep her."

"Her mother was a mess. It wasn't exactly a healthy home environment."

Finn leapt to his feet.

"You never gave her a chance to get better!" he spat. "You just acted, and you *destroyed* her; you destroyed her life. She's been a ghost ever since and you never even bothered to check in on her, to make sure she was okay; you just left her; you took her child and you left her."

Bruce opened his mouth to shout back but no words emerged. The anger just collapsed from his face and left only sorrow, and the fear he so guarded. Helen had hung her head into her hands and was weeping quietly. Finn could see teardrops sliding over and off her fingers. Bruce tried again to find his voice but when he failed, he slowly returned to his seat.

"When you say it like that, we sound like horrible people," Helen murmured, "but we did the best we could."

"For whom?"

Helen looked sharply up at him.

"You weren't there," she said. "You cannot understand the situation. It was a difficult decision for us but we were thinking only of Nicola."

"You can't say that," Finn told her levelly. "You changed her name to Nicola, Helen. That wasn't for her. Don't you feel guilty? I guess you do. You both took such care to set her up with money from the settlement. It was practically a pay off."

"She should have died in that accident," Bruce muttered.

Both Finn and Helen's eyes flashed wide with alarm.

"Bruce!" Helen hissed. "You don't mean that." She turned to Finn. "He doesn't mean that. He's just afraid. We both are. We've been waiting for this day to come for two years. We just don't want to lose her. I suppose that's why we never looked in on her. We were scared she'd be strong enough to take Nicola back."

Sympathy flaked into Finn's eyes.

"Why does that have to mean you're going to lose Nicola?" he asked softly. "She's your granddaughter and she loves you. I'm sure you've been loving guardians but it's not the same thing. It just isn't. Doesn't she deserve to know her mother?" Pain pinched his face and made his eyes shine. "Doesn't her mother deserve to get that chance?"

Helen's eyes suddenly widened.

"You love her," she realized.

Finn looked at her with a start but his disconcertion slid easily off his demeanor.

"Yes, I do," he said. "At least somebody does. At least she's not alone anymore, whether she wants to be or not."

"So, you're going to tell her," Bruce murmured.

Finn stared at him.

"Yes," he said.

"And what of *your* fear of losing *her*?" Bruce asked. "What happens when she remembers Robert? They loved each other."

Finn slowly shook his head.

"I'm still telling her."

"And if you lose her?"

He shrugged.

"That's up to her," he said. "That's always been up to her. There's nothing I can do about it and I'll love her regardless. Look, I'm going to tell her everything and I'm going to help her remember if I can. If you really want to do what's best for Nicola, and if you really want to stay in her life, you'll make this easy. I'm not trying to threaten you or anything. I just don't want any more pain."

Finn's eyes slowly wandered back towards the photograph on the mantle, towards the freeze frame of Roxanne's smiling face, her shining eyes, and agony split him apart. His vision blurred and blood rushed to his head and for a moment his composure foundered. When he wiped his eyes on the back of his hand, his knuckles came away wet.

"Please don't fight this," he said. "She has such a dark emptiness in her and she doesn't even know why, or what it was that once filled that place; that she has family. She's Nicola's mother. They need each other. *I* need her to be happy."

He looked back at Bruce. Bruce's gaze hovered in the glare of the large picture window that faced them and he seemed dazed.

Finn turned to Helen. Helen's eyes looked like glass and she stared at Finn without blinking.

"Just let them be together," Finn gently urged her. "I think if she remembers but you keep them apart, she's going to die."

He looked down at his watch. It was later than he thought. The weak sun would be gone completely in an hour.

"I have to go," he said. "But I'll be in touch."

He turned to leave, reached the foyer, but stopped, his hand on the inside wall of the sitting room. He looked back over his shoulder at Helen and Bruce.

"I don't want to lose her," he told them.

He dropped his hand and walked towards the door and as he grabbed the doorknob, Helen's voice reached out to him.

"Wait!"

Finn stopped and turned back as Helen caught up to him.

"Just wait," she said.

She disappeared up the stairs and returned a minute later with an envelope in her hand. It was folded in half and age had yellowed and creased it. She held it out to him.

"I'd like you to return these to her for me," she told him.

Finn took the envelope and anxiety scored Helen's face, her eyes following the wrinkled paper as it passed into his hands.

"Maybe they'll help her to remember," she said.

Finn looked down at the envelope. There was something small and hard inside. His brow furrowed but he didn't open it or ask what it was and Helen watched him slip the envelope into his coat pocket. He glanced up at her. She was wringing her hands in distress and Finn felt her sorrow like it was his own. Her fear made him afraid.

"Okay then," he murmured.

"Okay," Helen whispered.

He turned back to the door, pulled it open, and stepped outside. He hadn't realized his face was burning until the cold afternoon air washed across him and blistered the heat of his skin. He shut the door and hopped down the stairs and if he had turned back around he would have seen both Helen and Bruce watching him through the glare of the big picture window as he got into his car and left.

⟨ · ⟩

Finn pulled the car into the underground garage and parked. For several minutes he sat behind the wheel without moving, his eyes fixed on the bare, whitewashed, brick wall in front of him. Finally, he bit down on his bottom lip, reached into his coat pocket, and took out the envelope Helen had given him. He hesitated just a second longer before unfolding it and shaking its contents out on the palm of his hand.

The breath in his mouth evaporated.

A pair of plain, silver wedding bands gleamed up at him. The cold metal rings, polished to a watery luster, sent a shiver racing up his arm. One was larger than the other, a man's ring. The smaller ring was a woman's. The smaller ring was Roxanne's.

Finn stared at the wedding bands. He brushed his finger across them and they were icy to the touch. He picked up the smaller of the two and, in the dim, underground light, read the inscription on the inside of the band: *My one and only.*

Finn's eyes began to sting. His vision blurred and the delicately stenciled words in the inscription bled together. He looked away, into the rear view mirror where the mordant daylight was pushing strange, powdery shadows of itself through the sunken entrance of the underground parking lot, like translucent fingers trying to reach him in the darkness. He leaned his head back against the head rest and pressed his hands over his closed eyelids to shut out all the gloomy remnants of light and encapsulate himself in blackness. But he couldn't stop the images from running through his head. He saw again and again Roxanne's smiling face in that photograph. Inside his head she was in color. Her eyes glittered like ingots of fool's gold. The red strands in her brown hair snapped in the brush strokes of light the camera captured. Her milk skin glowed. The only emotion that stirred her was happiness.

He saw her staring up at him, her face in his hands, her eyes, those same glittering, golden eyes, so full and deep with wonder.

Her hair fanned out against her white pillow case like a glossy russet halo. He had ran his fingers through it until the sweat on the palms of his hands made it stand on end. Her face bleared in his gaze when he bent to kiss her. She had closed her eyes and kissed him back and when she cried, he had used his thumb to wipe the tears away. It had only lasted a few minutes, but the only emotion that had stirred her was happiness, fleeting but true.

He saw the mistrust when it slid serpent like back into her face, when it corrupted that brief joy. All the softness of her bearing had dissolved. Her eyes when she looked at him were hard and sharp as icicles, like touching her would break the skin. He couldn't remember the anger he had felt; he could only feel regret. He shouldn't have left her like that, with the passion he had stirred in her frozen over. It was like leaving her naked in the snow. If she regretted what happened between them, he felt that could kill him. He wanted most to make her smile again like she was forever smiling in that picture, forever beautiful; like she was forever happy.

Finn's eyes opened. His heart was racing but his dark irises were clear. His expression was hard with resolve. He slipped the rings back into the tattered envelope and the envelope back into his pocket. From the glove box, he fished out the folder Lewis had given him, tucked it under his arm, and left the car. His heart continued pounding as the webs of dying daylight disappeared completely.

Chapter Thirteen

Roxanne stood in the last strands of the waning sun, the cold wind stroking her face and throat like tiny needles as it tangled in her hair. She liked the roof. No one else ever came up there, so she knew no matter when she went she would be alone. She stood among the clustered rows of potted plants, most dead from the cold. It never occurred to her to put them in the greenhouse that stood empty behind them, even though she mourned them when they paled and withered. Some things weren't meant to grow in some times of the year. She could still tell what they were, even by the shriveled weeds they had become. The graves of roses were easy. The dead stalks still bore their thorns and she could spot the daisies like the parched soil still took to their blooms. They were like the tombstones of dear friends and she could sit beside them and remember them as they were.

Something flashed behind Roxanne's lidded eyes, a face so fleet it almost wasn't. The Ghost; the bleary apparition that kept her sleep restless and her open eyes blind. Then it was Finn who filled the spaces of her angst and it maddened her that he did, that he wouldn't leave her even when she was alone. Bitter tears sprang along her lashes and as she turned to leave, she almost didn't catch it. There, in the last pot, hidden behind the corpses of the others, a lone crimson bud had hatched from the briar of a dead rose.

Roxanne stared at it, daring not to blink lest it be only in her head. But it was real, wee and slight but strong and perfect, like someone had painted it. Two years had come and gone and this was the very first stroke of color she had seen. So long black and white in a world that is tormentingly not, this frail rose pearl was the most miraculous thing that had ever touched her frozen insides.

She knew it meant something. A plant doesn't grow in dead earth. She had let them wither on purpose in the first place so they wouldn't die was she to care for them. They weren't dead, only hibernating, only waiting for her to mend their outcast state.

Roxanne felt something wet on her cheeks and heavy hands brushed the tears from her face. She was angry at it, angry it hadn't gone away like everything else she must've had but couldn't hold onto. She wished the rose bud never was for now she wished it not to die.

Roxanne bent and plucked the clay pot up from the grime of the floor. Cradling it beneath her arm, she left the graveyard of the rooftop, a hand cupping the bauble of scarlet to protect it from the hackles of the wind. When she reached the stairwell, she pressed the pot against her ribs and wreathed her arms about its chalky basin as one would with an infant. She watched the rose bud as she navigated the steps. The inky bloom bobbed up and down to the rhythm of her feet. She thought she could see the color deepen, the silky petals unfurl, just at the warmth of coming inside.

Her eyes on the bud, she didn't see Finn crouching in wait by the door until she reached the landing, stepping across the berg of newspapers that was growing on the stoop of her neighbor's door. He rose to his feet when she neared and her face soured even as she felt her heart flutter like a butterfly on her ribcage. Finn carried beneath his arm a white folder with a yellowed envelope paper clipped to the top and his eyes were weary, as they were warm. The nearer she came to him the lower he felled his eyes, unable to match her own, and she was glad for it.

She stopped at the door and stared at the peep hole as he listed against the door frame, his eyes snagged on the frail blossom, its scarlet dye so stark against the dead skeleton of the rose bramble, like blood on snow.

"I don't think it's going to make it," he said.

Roxanne's tongue was sharp and swift.

"I'm sure everybody thought the same about you."

She could feel the thorns of her spurn hook his flesh like she had struck her own and, instantly, her voice softened, though she kept her eyes on the door in front of her.

"You know the door isn't locked," she said.

"I know," he murmured. "I wanted to wait for you."

Roxanne suddenly felt very aware of his eyes on her. He had seen her naked. He had heard her voice the moment of pleasure he had given her. He had stroked away the tears she had cried with his fingertips. He had seen her at her most unadorned, when there was no place left she could hide from him.

"Do you want to come in?" she asked.

She could feel Finn's faint smile.

"Yes," he said.

Roxanne opened the door and left it ajar at her back. Finn crossed the threshold behind her and shut the door as she set the clay pot down upon the kitchen counter and shrugged her coat from her shoulders.

She was still as she felt him near her, a hesitance in his manner that she didn't recognize.

"I'm sorry," he said, "about the other night. I don't think you're pathetic. I think you're really quite amazing. I still can't figure out why you chose me."

Roxanne whirled around to him, wrapping her arms about his neck and pressing her mouth over his. He fumbled in surprise for his feet and felt the wall at his back. The folder dropped from his hands as he wreathed his arms around her and leaned into her mouth. When she pulled away he had to gasp for air as he stared down on her in startle.

"I'm sorry," she murmured.

"Oh no," he said breathlessly. "Those kinds of surprises are good surprises."

Her eyes were dire as she anchored his gaze to hers.

"No, I'm sorry, Finn," she told him.

Finn brushed the hair from her face and laid his palm on her cheek.

"I know," he said.

A tear rolled off her lashes and purled over his fingers.

"I don't want to be alone anymore," she said. "I was fine before you. I could have done it. I could have been alone. It's like if you're born blind you never know what you're missing. But if you go blind, it's like torture. I can't be alone now, Finn, but that's not why, that's not the whole reason. What I feel, I don't know if I've ever felt. As far as I know, I've never been in love. But what I'm feeling, if I lose it, how could I forgive myself? I know I'm broken; I know I'm in pain, but when I'm with you, I don't feel it. When I'm with you, I like who I am. And I *hate* who I am. But you make me see what you see, like I'm watching everything through your eyes. For the first time I can see myself, Finn, and I can see that I need help. The past two years I have been a ghost... but I can start again, with you. I can learn myself again. I can stop mourning a past I don't remember and start making one I can. I can have memories; I can take pictures and hang them on the wall; I can stop grieving faces I've never seen, and names I've never heard, and places I've never known. I can start again right now. I can start like you were the beginning of my life; like I was only sleeping and you woke me up. And that is my past and that is all that matters. I remember you, Finn. You are my first memory."

Roxanne smiled, tasting salt on her lips, and felt her face dapple with hot dampness like summer rain. She couldn't meet his eyes; instead, wrapped her stare on his throat as it constricted and he struggled to snarl a voice. He was still for a long time and just as Roxanne's smile began to fade and the ills of sorrow well her eyes and bind her ribs taut, he laid both hands on the curves of her jaw and raised her gaze up into his own. His eyes were wet when she met them.

"You love me?" he asked.

Roxanne realized she had been holding her breath and released it in a serrated gale as her smile bloomed off her teeth and she laughed, tears rolling from her eyes into his hands like strands of pearls.

"I love you," she told him.

Finn pulled her into his arms and held her hard as he kissed her hair.

"Then, whatever comes next, I hope it's stronger," he said against her head.

There was a strange and bitter sorrow in his voice as his hands slid from her throat to her shoulders and he pushed her back to arms length.

"I have to talk to you," he said slowly.

Roxanne's mirth ebbed off her face at the torture in his eyes, a wicked dread snaking her spine.

"What is it, Finnean?" she murmured, shrugging out of his hands.

Finn felt her going cold as he retrieved the fallen folder from the floor and shuffled the papers back together. Roxanne's eyes were wary as she watched him.

"What is that?" she said, her stare webbed across the folder.

"It's you," Finn told her.

Roxanne narrowed her eyes, the perdition that hollowed her lungs drawing the blood from her face.

"I don't know how to do this," Finn said. "I assumed it would come to me in the moment but I don't know what I was thinking."

She was still, her gaze wide and filled like water balloons. Finn sighed deep and wearily and stroked a hand across his battered eyes.

"That scar on your abdomen," he told her, "I said it looked like a medical scar."

Roxanne was cold as stone and it wavered his nerve.

"Well, I know someone who owed me a favor and he gave me this," he said, tapping his fingers on the folder, "much to his own peril. I fought with myself about this, I really did. None of this matters to me. None of it changes who you are to me or that I love you. But it will change you. This is who you were, two years ago."

Roxanne's face had bled white, her eyes like two baubles of glass.

"You're not saying my name," she breathed, her voice tenuous, affrighted. "Why haven't you said my name?"

Sorrow coursed Finn's eyes.

"This isn't going to be easy to hear," he told her.

Roxanne was frozen where she stood.

"Just hurry up and say it because you're scaring me to death," she whispered.

Finn nodded and couldn't meet her stare.

"Your name isn't Roxanne," he told her.

His voice hit her like she had inhaled ice water.

"Your name is Rosamund," he said, his eyes on her hands, shivering listlessly at her sides. "LaMotte is your married name. Your maiden name is Orin. Rosamund Orin."

Roxanne's trembling hand hovered over the counter and leaned down upon it like it was the only thing holding her on her feet.

"But you remembered Roxanne," Finn said and he reared his eyes into hers. "Roxanne was your daughter's name."

The wells of Roxanne's eyes flooded and spilled over the rims of her lashes and all Finn could do for her was to go on.

"She was born four years ago, on the twenty-third of November," he said. "It was a cesarean birth. She was perfect, healthy, beautiful. Your husband, Robert, and his parents were your only family. You were an only child. Your mother raised you. You never knew your father. She died of cancer when you were nineteen. You married Robert LaMotte two years later and Roxanne was born a year after that. You named her after your mother. Do you ever wonder why you go to that park every Sunday? I think you took her there, every Sunday, rain or shine, like you still do. When Roxanne was not yet a year old you and Robert were in a car accident. It was horrific. Robert was killed instantly. You were in a coma for months and when you woke up, your daughter didn't know you. Your parents-in-law took her from you two years ago. I was thinking what kind of trauma it would take to steal your memory from you and losing your child after waking up to a dead husband would do it. This was the flat you shared with Robert and Roxanne. His parents took care of everything. Your money comes from the settlement from the accident. All your bills are paid through the bank. They set that up for you. Out of guilt or grief, I don't know. But they've been raising your daughter ever since. I don't know why they didn't wonder why you've never tried to contact them. They call her by her middle name now, Nicola."

Finn inhaled a deep, shuddered breath and let his iron taut shoulders slump.

"That's it," he said. "That's here."

He laid the folder on the counter and crossed his arms over his chest. He was slow to raise his eyes to hers. When he did, her face was stricken wet with tears and the hollow of her stare too deep for him to see the bottom. She looked as though he had dug into her chest, tore her heart out through the cage of her ribs and held it out in the palm of his hand for her to see it was still beating.

"Please say something," he whispered desperately.

Roxanne stared at him like he was a stranger.

"It isn't real," she breathed, her voice so frail he would not have caught it, had her lips not moved.

"It is," Finn told her. "You can read it for yourself."

Roxanne broke towards him, the nearer she became the deeper the fear in her eyes sank into her body.

"I don't know who Rosamund Orin is!" she told him fiercely, her voice suddenly solid as stone. "You're lying to me!"

"I'm not," Finn said swiftly, backing away towards the door as she advanced. "You're name is Rosamund Orin and you're a widow whose child was taken away."

"I don't remember any of what you've said!" she shouted, the heat of her nameless ire igniting her voice like an electrical charge.

"You could be feeding me some stranger's past. That's all it is to me. You could have made it up!"

"I thought you trusted me," Finn said, failing to stop the desperation from seeping into his demeanor. "It's all in your file. I took it from the hospital!"

Roxanne whirled and snatched the folder into her hands. She hurled it at him as she turned, its loose contents spilling as it cuffed his chest, and laid her trembling hands on the sides of his face.

"Why are you doing this?" she pleaded. "Why are you ruining this?"

"I'm trying to help you," he told her emphatically.

He tried to grasp her hands but when his fingers closed around hers she pulled them back and shrank away from him.

"Get out!" she cried, tears springing from her eyes.

"Rosamund—"

"Don't call me that!" she shrieked. Hysteria strangled her voice. "Get out, get out! Get out!!"

Agony swelled inside her and swallowed her voice back into her lungs, spilling from her eyes as it crackled against her ribs. Roxanne fell to her knees, her palms pressed over the burdened aching in her ribs.

"Get out..." she breathed, her voice shallow and splintered through the torrents she wept.

Finn felt his stare blear, felt it unraveling off his eyes as it took the words from his mouth and pushed him out the door. He would not repent, but he would mourn her leaving him.

Chapter Fourteen

Roxanne fought. Crumpled on the floor, her knees too weak to carry her, the well of her eyes had dried up. So heavy were her eyelids, so raw and worn, she could not keep them open. She listed against the side of the counter and did not stir, though behind her shuttered stare she wailed against the walls of her own mind to remember something, anything.

But Roxanne's mind was like a black hole. Everything she fed got swallowed up. She felt the pressure of her thrashing to remember boiling the blood between her brow and her skull. But what Finn had said was poison, another person's tragedy she could tell herself was sad but that meant nothing to her.

She would know if she had a child. She would know if she was a mother. Things like that are buried deeper in the human consciousness, tattooed inside the soul. She would know.

Before it crossed her mind, Roxanne found the name in her mouth.

"Rosamund Orin," she breathed. It was a stranger's name.

"Roxanne LaMotte."

The name rolled from her tongue as though she had said it a thousand times. It was not a name she knew, not her own, but it made a kind of bitter sense, like missing puzzle pieces turning up long after the puzzle has been forgotten.

She wanted to remember now, as much as she was afraid to.

The hospital folder still lay by the door, its leafy contents strewn out around it like a fan. She could see the corner of a photograph sticking out beneath the generic petals of paper and she pushed herself away from the counter toward it. She knelt at its edge and slid the photo from beneath the leaves, holding it up to her eyes with both hands.

It was a picture of a car accident, of two vehicles. One had slammed into the driver's side of the other. The metal shells were twisted and mauled, the glass shattered over the pavement like flecks of silver snow.

Roxanne stared at it, long until it stung her eyes, and she laid it back upon the floor.

It's going to rain...

It was a voice inside her head, soft and faraway, a man's voice. It startled her and froze her still as stone.

"No it isn't," she said out loud, the words wooden and rehearsed on her tongue. "Don't say that..."

A man's face flashed over her eyes, the ghost inside her head. He was beside her. He turned his head and smiled at her.

What will you do if it does...?

Roxanne's eyes welled, the face blearing in her mind, the voice echoing off the shadows.

"If the sky cries, then so will I," she whispered, another voice, frail and distant, saying the words along with her inside her head.

It was her own voice.

She heard the man laugh.

"Watch the road," Roxanne breathed.

Her fingers brushed against the wrinkled envelope. She looked down at it and used her fingertips to draw it to her side. For a minute she just stared at it and felt along the circular ridges of what was inside. She picked it up, unfolded the flap, and shook out the two wedding rings into her hand. The silver bands caught the light and her heart stopped with a hiccup and a rush of blood to her head.

A man's face flooded her mind. He was handsome, with bright eyes and thick hair she got a flashed image of running her hands through. Her heart began to throb and she picked up the larger of the two rings and held it up to the overhead kitchen light. She slowly turned it to read the inscription and tears bubbled into her eyes.

"My one and only," she read. Her eyes flew wide and she clamped a hand across her mouth. "Oh my god."

She remembered strong arms holding her, her heart beating fast, soft lips on her neck, the scratch of stubble.

She gasped.

"Robert!" She took the smaller band and slid it onto the ring finger of her left hand. It fit perfectly. "These were ours," she breathed. "These were yours and mine."

A blithe smile peppered her face but only for a second, before a chasm of despair opened up within her and swallowed that brief serenity of remembrance whole. Her body trembled as she removed the ring and set it down with its pair.

The face was fading off her eyes, like a shape slipping into the fog, and a sudden agony tore into Roxanne's heart. She felt cold tears weeping down the heat of her face and the nothingness that filled her head now was different to the nothingness of the last years. She brought her shivering fingers up to her brow and drew them through the tangles of her hair until she felt her skull on her fingertips. She was trembling as she traced the long, splintered scar that etched her flesh from her hairline to the back of her ear. Her head had hit the window. The glass had shattered over her.

"Where is Robert....?"

A baby was crying.

Roxanne turned her eyes and for the palest moment the flat behind her was washed in warm, honey-colored light.

"She won't eat her peas," a voice said before a barren darkness swathed the room again.

"She'll eat them if I feed her," Roxanne whispered.

Roxanne laid her palms on the floor and pushed herself to her feet, her limbs shuddering as though all the heat in her body had evaporated. She reached out and hooked the handle of the kitchen drawer into her hand. She wrenched back on it and it gave with sudden swiftness. The drawer shot open and its contents spilled to the floor as it turned over in her fingers, the handle fixed in her fist. A cluster of dusty, metal spoons clattered over the floorboards.

Roxanne leaned the drawer against the counter and bent down to them. She stirred her fingertips through the cold, metal stalks until they glided across something that froze the breath in her mouth and stopped her heart. It was a small, plastic spoon, narrow and thick, its end bubbled like the tiny half of a clamshell. It was bright purple and dappled with yellow flowers that had begun to fade.

The well behind Roxanne's eyes surged and overflowed her lashes.

"Roxie Loxie," she cried. Her feet slipped out from beneath her. "That's what I called you."

The beautiful agony of lifelong memories flooded her head like the bursting of a dam and they were hers.

She remembered everything.

Chapter Fifteen

It seemed like Finn had been staring at the phone an eternity. The worn slip of paper was folded in one hand though he didn't need it. He knew Peter's number by heart, though he had never once dialed it.

He couldn't hold her anger against her. It was fear and he knew it as his own. How could he expect her to face her trepidation was he not to purge his own? How could he be disappointed she was afraid?

Before he let his mind wander into the maze it was, Finn punched the numbers off his fingertip and pushed the phone to his ear. While the line sang, the only reason he didn't hang up was because he was paralyzed where he stood and Peter's voice hit him like a wayward football to his gut. Ingrained with static and faraway, the answering machine met his ear.

"You've reached Peter, Sarah, and the girls. Call us back or leave a message."

Finn felt a grievous berg of sorrow choke his throat and push tears against the rims of his eyes. The voice was so stale, so mechanical and rehearsed, yet he knew it, the same way a certain aroma can recall memories long forgotten.

When the machine chirped, Finn panicked to find he had swallowed his voice and he fought to net it back onto his tongue.

"Hey, Peter," he said, clearing his throat. "It's me... It's Finn. Don't get excited. I just thought we could get a cup of coffee or something. Maybe I could meet Sarah and your girls...."

Finn's voice floundered, like the lungs of a drowning man. He could feel his lashes growing sopped and heavy and shielded his eyes beneath a hand as he inhaled a deep and shuddering breath.

"I don't know," he said, the words shaking on his tongue. "Something's happened to me. I shouldn't be trying to pretend you're something you're not, or you're not something you are... Anyway. I don't know what else to say. None of us are who we were once... That's it, I guess... I'll see you...."

Finn's hand wavered before he disconnected. When he hung up, the silence that followed was like the haunted stillness after church bells cease their chorus, like the hollowness in the air left behind the great, overwhelming sound.

Finn's entire being was lighter. He was floating up on the ocean and didn't care that the tide was drawing him further and further from the shore. There was nothing beneath him and only sky above him and everything or nothing was possible.

The frail knock that sparked against his door startled him. For a moment he didn't move, was frozen still where he stood as though the soles of his feet had sprouted roots. The thought of leaving it unanswered crossed his mind but was quickly abandoned as he stirred over the threshold.

When he opened the door, she looked almost surprised.

Roxanne's eyes were glassy and red, her face pale and raw from crying. Her entire body trembled and she held her hands pressed against her chest as though she feared her heart would slip though her ribs.

The moment they drew their eyes together seemed to last longer than the second it really did.

Roxanne's breath shivered from her open mouth as though she couldn't catch enough air to quench her lungs.

"I... I have a daughter," she said, her eyes filling and spilling as she listened along to the words she spoke out loud.

Finn felt his heart break for her and he reached out and pulled her to him. She stepped willfully into the bough of his arms and wept onto his shoulder as he held her, her breath hot on his neck.

"Will you help me find her?" she cried, her shivering hands at his back gathering his shirt into her fists.

Finn smiled against the tangles of her hair and nodded his head.

"Yes," he told her, "I will."

They didn't know how long they stood there in the skeleton of Finn's door, their arms about each other, never to let go again, even when they would. But before the day had ended, Roxanne asked Finn if they could be forgiven and if he would begin to call her Rosamund.

He answered yes and yes.

Chapter Sixteen

As they drove, she kept her eyes on the window beside her, on the world that bleared by beyond it. She had bitten each fingernail down to the quick and she felt a pulsating lump in her throat. Only Finn beside her gave the courage to her nerve that kept away the ravenous tides of fear.

"She'll not know you, Rosamund," he said.

She turned her head and looked to him, his gaze steeled on the road in front of them.

"She wasn't yet two years old the last time she saw you."

He had been saying so for days, if only to prepare her.

"I know," she told him, "I remember." Rosamund turned back to the window. "But she is still my daughter and I am still her mother. Time can't disfigure that."

Finn pulled to the side of the road. Rosamund watched him, perdition furrowing her brow, as he shut off the engine and slowly returned her stare.

"We're here," he said and stirred his gaze beyond her out the window.

A large brick building stood across from the car on the other side of the road, a penned playground beside it brimming with children and parents.

"This is it?" she asked, her voice tight with anxiety, though she knew that it was.

Finn leaned nearer to her to survey the playground.

"Pre-school's just let out," he told her.

He opened the door and got out, standing in its gape for a better look, a hand resting on the roof of the car. Rosamund slowly followed him, listlessly pushing the door away from her.

Finn narrowed his eyes over the crowd.

"I don't see..."

Hanging half way out of the car, Rosamund suddenly stopped, the vast gape of her stare snagged by someone in the crowd. Everything around her froze for that brief moment it took for her to know she was hers.

A little girl, clad in a pixie sized school uniform, was hopping over the splinters in the stone walkway. Her face was pale and bright, her hair dark and tangled with glossy curls, russet-colored like Rosamund's own.

But that was not what mapped her veins hot and cold all at once. It was the tiny spark in the cold places of her heart, a frail feeling of familiarity, though she didn't know the child. But of all the faces that had passed her by, only this one did she know was hers.

All the demons in her soul were fled, all the shadows soaked in light, her fears ebbed like poison from a wound. All that remained, a kinetic harmony, like all the world's billions of tenors were singing to the same ballad, in the same key, for the first time.

"I see her," she whispered, her voice frail as all her mettle went to staving off the torrents that abraded her irises.

Finn caught and followed her line of sight as Rosamund slowly got out of the car to her feet, her hands bitten with cold and shivering, though her face burned. He saw the little girl, skipping through the stalks of grown-ups. Someone snagged her hand and drew her near.

"You're right," he said, knowing she didn't need his validation, knowing it was only for himself. "Those are Robert's parents with her, Helen and Bruce."

Rosamund didn't see them. She didn't take her eyes from the child, afraid now to lose her in the crowd, afraid now she was only in her head, wanting so desperately that she be real that it ached her skin.

Finn snaked around the car and laid his hand on top of her own, shackled to the top of the door.

"She'll still be there," he murmured.

Rosamund slowly stroked her eyes to his and he brushed the hair from her face and kissed her brow. She tried to say 'thank you' but the words drowned in her throat. Thank you wasn't enough; it couldn't encompass what she had inside for him. He couldn't understand the bounds of devotion that were his, her heart that was his for what he had given her. She loved him, not for what she had lost that she had found, but for the hope of what they would make together, such hope as she had never felt before.

And as he held her, so near she could feel the beating of his heart inside her own, she knew she had the chance of the rest of their lives to show him she was who he believed she would become.

Finn brushed his mouth over hers, stroked the strands of tears from her cheeks with soft fingertips, and whispered in her ear, "She's been waiting for you."

Rosamund slowly turned back to the crowd. Finn's palm on her back gently spurred her feet and they crossed the road together, her heart braying so loud off the walls of her head it smothered all else in her ears. They stopped on the edge of the sidewalk, where the parents were slowly gathering up their children, and the crowd seemed to part for them until there was left an emptied path that lead only to her.

Helen and Bruce saw her first and there was no trace of startle in their eyes. They looked on Rosamund and their eyes were filled with grim, but decided, acceptance.

But she did not return them. Her stare was rapt upon the girl who felt the heaviness in the air and followed the gazes of her grandparents. When she saw Rosamund and smiled, shy and innocent as children do, Rosamund felt her heart stop and her breath catch on her ribs, like she feared she was invisible.

She felt Finn beside her, his hand on her spine, softly pushing her feet, and she impelled forward. It took all the strength she had to restrain what raged to be undone just behind her eyes. As she neared, she felt her legs were going to fail her and foundered to a knee, a hand plastered over her mouth.

"Hi, sweetheart," she whispered with a deep breath through the bars of her fingers.

Nicola hesitated a moment, her eyes wide and chary, then wrested out of Helen's hand and slowly came towards her.

Terrified to move and startle the girl, Rosamund held her breath.

"Do you know me?" she asked, her voice slivered.

Nicola tilted her head and Rosamund could feel the deep of her eyes watching the curves and shadows of her face. And Rosamund was awestruck.

"Are you my mummy?" Nicola asked.

Rosamund laughed as the well of her eyes flooded and purled off her lashes, her breath returning to her lungs in a sudden gale. Such exquisite agony, she had never known.

"Why are you crying?" Nicola asked.

Rosamund's smile was so wide it ached the corners of her mouth.

"I'm just so happy to see you," she said, tasting tears on her lips.

"You've been away a long time," Nicola told her.

"Yes, I have," Rosamund said, drawing her fingers over her cheeks as she nodded. "But I'm here now and I'm not going to go away ever again."

Nicola nodded earnestly and raised a hand to Rosamund's face, sopping up a stray tear with her fingertip.

"You missed one," she said.

Rosamund laughed again, if only to keep from weeping.

"Thank you, Nicola," she breathed. "Thank you."

From her back, Finn watched them, his gaze wandering once to meet Helen's and Bruce's. He smiled very faintly at them, with very real sympathy and very real hope. Bruce's eyes were still hard as stone but Helen returned his tenuous smile. They were going to try and Finn was grateful to them for that.

Finn reveled in the embattled happiness he felt from Rosamund, his heart in his throat to watch her finding herself again. All the time that had separated them, all the things she had missed, melted away and they were left with only now and only what would be. Rosamund had died to be so near to home. She never thought that it was here with the earth beneath her feet.

It was the future Rosamund had forgotten. Her past was always with her. Though she could not remember it, it never left her. And still, what would become was not what mattered; it was whose hand she held when she arrived.

LaVergne, TN USA
04 March 2010

174995LV00002B/3/P